Trekking On A Human Landscape

Joseph Morin

Published by Joseph Morin, 2021.

TREKKING ON A HUMAN LANDSCAPE

First edition. February 9, 2021.

Copyright © 2021 Joseph Morin.

ISBN: 979-8201637897

Written by Joseph Morin.

To the many individuals who inspired the characters in these
works of fiction.

Introduction

These works of fiction emerged from non-fictional events experienced by the author. Each short story is intensely human. Join these unique characters while they meander through the ordinariness of their lives, stumbling upon sadness, irony, humor, regret, shame or loss—the parts that make us all human.

1. *Who Was Gordy?* is a story of lost identity where a quirky character, Gordy, is encountered later in life by the narrator who knew Gordy as a trash collector in his old neighborhood while he was growing up. Gordy, now much older, has lost what he once had but sadly, falsely feels he can still be that person for one lingering moment.

2. *Reverent for The Day* is a story about altered perceptions. It's the narrator's wedding day and he finds the tuxedo he rented, doesn't fit. This predicament unavoidably immerses him in accepting assistance from an unlikely source. Through this encounter he is forced to confront that his long-held perceptions of a person he once feared, were not what they seemed to be. The ambiguity of his doctrinaire upbringing in the Catholic Church and his current status of being a bit of an 'outsider' is troubling for him.

3. *When Quinn Was Not Himself* is a humorous account of a case of mistaken identity. In this story, two narratives converge at a weekend watercolor workshop put on by a local art museum. The collision of Quinn's misrepresented status as a painter and the lofty ambitions of young intern provide an hilarious account of a plan gone very wrong.

4. In *News From Meaford* two brothers separated at a young age by family tragedy are reunited. The alchemy of bad news and righting wrongs provides for a kind of awakening in the older

brother. Sadly, it is too late.

5. *The Old Man Who Came Late,* is a story that takes place at a film festival in a small college town. A young film-maker produces a controversial film about an imposter who scandalized the University years ago by successfully duping the administration into hiring him as the Chair of the Psychology Department. The showing of the film has aroused the interest of an eclectic group consisting of former students of the imposter, former colleagues, and newer students, separated from the story by a couple of generations. Mysteriously, one other attendee arrives a bit late, an older man who has a special interest in the film.

6. *Liar, Liar, Pants on Fire* is a story of a seemingly well-intentioned counsellor who feels its his duty to disclose a young student's lie. His surprise visit ends up revealing, not his student's lie but a deeper truth. The irony is palpable.

7. *The Empty Seat* involves a moment in the life of a man named Ron who has cerebral palsy. Readers get a glimpse of what it is like to live in a body racked with involuntary movements but the story is deeper than that. Ron's older brother has provided him with a bunch of tickets to a hockey game. The event has a *One Flew Over the Cookoo's Nest* feel to it. The interactions of the diverse group of characters (Ron's roommates) contrasts starkly with the uncomfortableness of Ron's able-bodied volunteer, Trevor, as he awkwardly navigates a very emotional evening. It is a story about loss and aloneness.

Who Was Gordy?

There was a faint familiarity about him that caught me.

"Who's that?" I asked while sipping a warm beer.

"Who? Oh. That's Gordy ...Aunt Milly's new B-O-Y friend."

I offered a brief smirk acknowledging Jerry's sarcasm but said nothing. Jerry and I were at a party, one that I didn't want to go to. Jerry didn't either, though the party was for his mother's 60th birthday. It was one of his Aunt Milly's crusades to prop up the rickety façade of their fractured family. *Forced fraternizing* Jerry called it.

"Winnie will be pissed he's here," Jerry whispered. Jerry's mother's name was actually Elizabeth but he had called her *Winnie* for as long as I'd known him. Not in her presence though.

Gordy. I kept mumbling his name while watching from across the room. His excesses drew me in more as I plumbed the depths of my memory. His voice. His actions. Nothing about him was subtle. All resonating with my past. Finally it came to me. Sure! It was Gordy alright!

Gordy hadn't seemed to have changed much from when I was a kid. I would have been about ten at the time. He was still as wiry as he was then. His hair still long, although no longer blonde. It was more grey than blonde and greased back not quite hiding patches of bare scalp. He was even shorter than I remembered. His well-shined cowboy boots gave him an extra inch or so. He had on a garishly loud shirt. It was one of those Hawaiian jobs, not well suited for the cold snap we were experiencing. The top two buttons were undone—his bony chest peeked through the thin fabric like exposed springs from a well-worn car seat. His glasses were the same as I remembered too—oddly thick, distorting his eyes to twice their size like an exotic fish peering out from a waiting-room aquarium. A prominent gold necklace strained from the heft of the gold cross attached to it. It was too yellowy to be real gold. The size of it seemed to compete with his diminutive frame, as if he might topple over with its weight. His odd appearance had a remarkable congruence with my memory of him way back then.

Gordy was from my old neighborhood. He had been a trash collector and his route took him on to our street. It was Gordy's oddness and not his employment that ensured recollection...even after some thirty-odd years. In my mind's eye I could still see him with his shirtsleeves rolled up high, the way tough-guys used to do it. An ever-present package of Camel's peeked over the brim of his shirt pocket. His coke-bottle thick glasses were held in place with binder twine, tufting his hair on the back making it stick up like the spritely tail of a small dog. A gold filling in his front tooth gave him a pirate-like quality. Ridiculous? Maybe, but when you are ten, ridiculousness can be sublime.

To his fellow workers he must have been an obnoxious buffoon—someone to be endured and not much else. But not to us. To us he was a delightful interlude, briefly suspending the boredom of a sweltering summer day. He had a panache about him that sucked in attention. We always dropped what we were doing and watched, mesmerized by his antics. Gordy would hang precariously off the back of the truck while it lurched from house to house. He would reach way out, latch on to a can with one hand while the truck was still in motion and then use his other arm as a kind of hinge, slinging the can high onto the truck where another man would catch it. These cans, bulging with kitchen waste, could be monstrously heavy and yet he was so small! He was daring too. Instead of stepping off the truck like the other men, he would execute a perfect front flip, always landing on his feet. No one we knew could do this. We were amazed.

"Watch this kids!" he would boast while performing another flip. "Good eh?" boldly fishing for praise. As impressionable children, humility was not a quality we understood so no scorn was directed at him for his brag. What he could do was indeed 'good'.

His revered stature didn't hold up for long though. I remember he would laugh—a laugh much louder than it needed to be...a kind of clown's laugh. There was something hidden behind it...something sad...something untold. Although I had no worldly experience to explain it, I knew enough to know his laughter probably came from a place devoid of humor.

With the party underway I made my way over to him. He donned a suspicious grin, his gold-filled tooth winking back at me from behind tobacco-stained teeth. It was definitely him. Our initial conversation was labored at first as I found him quite guarded. I felt myself having to convince him that my memories contained nothing he should be ashamed of. Moments of awkwardness sputtered along until the mention of his acrobatics. It was then that a threshold was crossed enabling me to nudge a more spirited response from him. His enthusiasm bubbled to the surface. I became a bit troubled by the magnitude of it. His wide-eyed grin did not match the mild praise I was plying. His eyes began to flash with unwarranted excitement. Foolishly I continued to stoke his ego with more child-spawned admiration. Until I recognized my cordialness had exceeded its purpose. I retreated and abruptly changed the subject. "So what are you up to now Gordy?" Unfortunately, this had no impact. His metamorphosis continued unabated. Clearly, he had latched on to his revived identity. Thoughts began to pop up like targets in a shooting gallery. What had I done?

"I still can do that!"

Did he mean his front flip? I thought.

As I looked into his bulging eyes, quite distorted from the thick lenses, I could see my own reflection mirrored back to me. He was seeing me as I am I thought, but I, only the distortion of his magnified eyes. I was looking at a curiosity while he was seeing an admirer. Shame seeped into the moment like smoke under a shut door. I could not un-ring the bell I had just rung.

"Watch!" he trumpeted.

He began nudging people aside, pushing chairs closer to the table where the refreshments were. Since no one but me knew the conversation that prompted his movements, puzzled guests looked on with a restrained curiosity. Sitting close to the refreshment table, Milly was encouraging her sister to open the few gifts plainly arranged around the yellow cake. Becoming aware of the distraction, she stopped what she was saying mid-sentence and locked on to her boyfriend. Her expression abruptly changed from mild amusement to a white-hot flash of contempt.

"Gordy! Stop! No. Not ...not here!" she pleaded.

Finally recognizing what he was about to attempt, I furiously tried to persuade him differently. With a violent grunt, Gordy launched himself into the air, somersaulting high enough for his head to clear the floor but sadly not enough to have his feet land as they should. There was a moment of suspended animation as Gordy hovered while using his legs to cantilever his body in a hopeless attempt to keep him from falling to the floor. With a fierce urgency he grabbed the nearest chair, desperately trying to break his fall. It held him for a brief moment but eventually it toppled over, catapulting the refreshment table a full three feet into the air. Gordy crashed on to the floor with the simultaneous arrival of exploding cake and pulp-filled fruit punch right onto the shocked faces of both Milly and her sister. A chorus of screams followed and then a sudden silence punctuated the moment. A few reluctant ice cubes slowly lost their grip on the plastic table cloth and fell to the floor with a muted clink. Gordy was groaning. He had hurt himself. How badly? It was not apparent. No one came to his rescue. They let him lay there ... as did I.

The frozen moment allowed people to take stalk. Gordy continued to push out incomprehensible utterances. His glasses were a few feet away. One of his thick lenses had dislodged from its frame. His necklace, now twisted in a half-loop, draped ignominiously over his head. A sticky blob of yellow icing clung to the gold cross.

Milly managed a few nervous giggles but then stopped abruptly. Eventually guests scurried to pick up displaced objects. Milly's daughter went for a mop. I stooped down to prop Gordy up and retrieve his glasses for him. There he squatted in the detritus. He sat there, hollowed out like the rotting rind of a fallen log, a fading effigy of what once was. His one decaying attribute had abandoned him. Who was he now?

Reverent For the Day

My memories of the room had jiggled since I had last been here. Things felt diffuse and out of place. I had to concentrate to get my bearings. The Sacristy of the old church seemed not as grand as I remembered. Its contents as well—the bureau less high, the Episcopal chair less majestic, the vestment cupboards less ornate, the large center table less large, and the light streaming through the elegant stained-glass window, less enchanting. Even the usual spicy scent of lemon oil on the furniture smelled dusty and old. The feeling of being unwelcome though, that had not changed.

Today is my wedding day. The tuxedo I rented doesn't fit right. The pants are at least six inches too long. The mistake, unfortunately, was not discovered until this morning while Richard and I nursed our hangovers.

"Shit! Look at this! They're too fucking long." I glanced at Richard's. "Your's fit perfectly!" Richard's uproarious reaction to the two of us standing in front of the mirror in his basement apartment, with my pant legs flopping around like a circus seal, confirmed that I had just added to his expansive inventory of what he called 'Phil's Famous Flounders'. "What the hell am I going to do? We should'a tried them on."

Richard, trying to hold back a smirk managed to push out, "We need pins!" between spasms of snorting.

I looked at him with blank disappointment. "That's brilliant. I can see why I picked you to be my Best Man."

Richard absorbed the sarcasm and offered nothing in response. *Where could we get pins in this short amount of time?* It might have been our ignorance of where tailoring supplies could be purchased but it was more likely due to the residue of last night's gin still sloshing around in our brains that couldn't bring a workable solution to the surface.

Eventually a few reluctant neurons were revived enough to conceive the plan that brought me here.

"Vestments!" I exclaimed. "Priests keep a ton of pins for their vestments."

So we set out for the church an hour early, with Richard neatly dressed in his tux and me in a pair of jeans with my rented pants in hand. The merit of the plan was initially promising but my optimism began to fade in the short ride over to the parish Rectory. It would seem the few minutes of stewing over my predicament allowed some dormant insecurities to be exhumed.

"What'll I say?" I mumbled.

"Whad'ya mean what'll you say? Tell them you need to borrow some pins!" Richard directed as he pulled up to the curb in front of the church.

"Yeah but...it'll be humiliating."

Richard placed his arm over the back of the seat and shook his head slowly. He had that *not-this-again* look. It annoyed me that my boyhood lamentations could still have such a grip on me even after all these years. "There's old Phil" I began to rant. "...messed up again... Remember when he was daydreaming and rang the Consecration Bells at the wrong time? ...How about when he burned a hole in the Bishop's brand new crimson carpet with hot wax from the acolyte candle, BECAUSE HE DIDN'T TIE HIS SHOE LACES! That was a doozie! Could'a burned the damn place down...Never thought the Bishop would get over that one!" I went through a litany of blunders, each one resulting in Bishop Morocco's searing admonishment. I ended with, "Worst altar boy there ever was...too bad he wasn't more like David Young!"

"David Young?"

"Yeah. He was the Bishop's favorite...wanted to become a priest."

"Ah. I see. Anyway, that was a long time ago." Assuaging was Richard's specialty. "Besides, how do you know he's still here?"

"Who...Morocco? He's still here alright." Glancing back to the Rectory, "I asked when we booked the church for the wedding." Thinking about this a bit more I added. "...nearly changed my mind when I heard though."

Richard grinned and held it for a few seconds. I made no motion for the door handle. The two of us sat contemplating what would come next. Richard broke the silence. "Whad'ya say to that new priest ...the one who's marrying you...Saba what's-his-name?"

"Sabistini. Father Sabistini," I corrected. "Whad'ya mean whad I say?"

"He musta asked you when you made th'rangements? You know...when he asked about your faith and sin...all that religious bull shit?"

"What was I supposed to say? I haven't gone to church in years? I've committed so many sins since my last confession I'd have to take up residence in the confessional for months? ...told him I was a practicing Catholic...jus bin away for a while...you know...out of town. What else was I going to say?"

Richard smiled, obviously enjoying my state of moral entrapment. He continued to pester me. "You go to confession?"

I hesitated before answering knowing where the conversation was headed.

"Yeah?"

"Whud'ya confess?"

"Never mind what I confessed...none of your damn business."

Richard's eyes sparkled mischievously. Leaning in toward me he said with a wink, "Maybe I should ask, what didn't ya confess eh?" He jabbed me in the ribs.

I looked at my watch. "Let's get on with this. We're run'in oud'a time."

I remembered the sound the door chime made—its rich deep tone conveyed the weight of the pipes without actually seeing them—three welcoming notes, pleasant to some maybe but hearing them again was unsettling. The early morning servers would have to ring the chime to wrest Mrs. Gilchrist from her cooking chores in the Rectory kitchen. It signaled her to unlock the side entrance to the Sacristy so they could prepare the altar for the 7:30 mass—the Bishop's mass.

Nothing. I pushed the doorbell again. Eventually there were footsteps. A moment of fidgeting with the locking mechanism suggested someone unfamiliar with the behavior of the door's latches would be greeting us. Finally, the heft of the great door began to move. I was not prepared for our greeter.

"Your Excellency!"

The shock of seeing Bishop Morocco was magnified by his state of undress. He wore black pants, ones usually associated with the clergy, but no shirt, only a sleeveless undershirt. A dollop of shaving cream clung to his left ear lobe. A small towel was draped over his right shoulder. His thin arms protruded comically from his undershirt, like hairy pipe-cleaners.

"Yes?" He asked.

Sputtering inanely, I began. "I was...that is...uh...is Mrs. Gilchrist around by any chance?"

"No." he said blankly. "It's Saturday." He paused. "She shops for the Rectory on Saturday," saying it as if her schedule was common knowledge.

"Oh uh. That's a...that's a shame. Uh...any idea when she will be back?"

"Around one o'clock, I - would - think?", slowing the pace of the last few words.

That would be well after the wedding ceremony. I looked back at Richard hoping that in the few moments that had elapsed he would be inspired by a new solution to my problem. His resigned expression however suggested that I shouldn't expect any inspiration from him. I looked back at the Bishop. I was operating from what I perceived to be a slim advantage—the possibility he may not have recognized me from my altar boy days. Feeling rather intrepid, I felt safe in disclosing an element of my predicament.

"Your Excellency," I sounded excessively reverent—too pleading. I ratcheted it back. "I would like to borrow some pins." I didn't want to give him much more than that. "I thought Mrs. Gilchrist might be able to get me a few from the Sacristy?"

The Bishop hesitated for a second and then nudged the bridge of his glasses with his finger, adjusting them as if to get a better view of me.

"Pins? Why would you need pins?"

I paused. At this point I wanted to retreat although I had no idea of what I would do instead. The Bishop was my only hope. "Well your Excellency I'm kind of in a jam. We...I'm getting married today ...in about forty minutes actually, and uh...my pants...I rented a tuxedo and the pants are too long...much too long." I looked at Richard. He nodded in affirmation. Looking back at the Bishop, I expected a clarifying question to follow. None came so I repeated my request. "We thought there might be some pins in the Sacristy we could...I could use."

An uncomfortable few moments hung in the air as I waited for the Bishop to consider the situation. His expression conveyed a struggle between pity and intense disappointment. He glanced at Richard and then back at me before asking the obvious. "You didn't try them on ahead of time?" he questioned. *There was that tone again.* I didn't answer. With my ardor wilting I managed only a pathetic wince in response. After several painful moments, he stated bluntly, "I'm in the middle of getting dressed. You'll have to wait." Pulling the door wider he gestured us to enter.

We waited in the foyer as directed while he continued with his morning shave. After about fifteen minutes we heard a door shut. Soon the Bishop descended the stairs. The stairway had a ninety degree turn halfway up. A small landing provided the transition from one flight to the next. The Bishop stopped on the landing momentarily and looked down at us as if he was still contemplating whether to help. He was dressed in his bishop's robes with the familiar black cassock elegantly embroidered in fine silk with crimson piping along the edges. A scarlet sash was belted tightly to his waist while a length of it draped down vertically to the bottom of his cassock. A large cross hung from his neck suspended by a sturdy gold chain. His red silk skullcap fit snuggly to the bald spot on his thinning hair. His left hand held a well-scuffed black prayer book while his right gripped the banister. I could see the gold Episcopal ring with its immense stone—its lustrous violet hue winking in the morning sunlight cascading through the vestibule window. *I kissed that ring* I thought. I locked onto a memory from my elementary school days when the Bishop was being introduced for the first time as our new pastor. It was quite an honor. Never before had a bishop been appointed a pastor to a church in our diocese. In preparing us to greet him appropriately, Sister Mary Rita instructed us to address him as *Your Excellency* and to kiss his ring if he should put out his hand. I recall being a bit hesitant about the ritual but abruptly changed my mind when Dougie McCaffrey whispered the titillating notion that the gem was the kind that you could only find in a pirate's treasure chest.

"Come," he said while taking the last few steps. Without a modicum of conviviality, he added, "We'll go to the Sacristy".

He led us through the big kitchen to a door that opened to the hallway that eventually connected to the Sacristy. On the way, the Bishop paused by the stairway leading down to the change room where the altar boys put on their vestments. He looked at me expectantly. My puzzled expression elicited an impatient frown from him. "You'll need to put them on, won't you?"

"On? Oh the pants...yes...I see. Sure...the change room. I'll be right back." *What was he planning? All I wanted was pins. Did he know that I would know where the altar servers changed?*

The old wooden cupboards where the black cassocks and the white surplices were stored lined the far wall just as I remembered. The cupboard doors were still marked by the letters *S*, a slightly askew *W*, and an *L* for small, medium and large. The *W* was actually a *M* turned on its side when the nail on top of it failed. Pressed for time I didn't waste a moment taking my jeans off and putting on the tuxedo pants. I quickly rolled them up so that I wouldn't trip on the stairway leading to the hallway where the Bishop and Richard were waiting. I had no idea what they talked about in my absence but Richard looked very uncomfortable.

Once in the Sacristy the Bishop made his way to the bureau with its many wide drawers. There were several of them, all quite shallow for holding individulal vestments that the clergy wore when performing sacred duties. There were rituals and prayers associated with each and I could recall the Bishop attaching great significance to both the sequence and the level of private contemplation prescribed for every one of them. As a young boy, I was charmed by the discipline of the routine and its intense preparation. I recall moments of imaginative play where I would secretly simulate my own dressing ritual, as if I were the Bishop presiding at a mass—calling into service such things as a scarf, a brimless ball cap, and a discarded sheet to drape over my shoulders. One of my mother's silver wine goblets was conscripted to become a sacred chalice, employing apple juice for wine and mushed up discs of white bread for the Eucharist. Of course, nothing resembling piousness took root and as with other youthful exuberances, adolescence quickly provided me with life's other options. The attraction of becoming a man of the cloth vanished without a trace.

The Bishop placing his prayer book on the bureau began rummaging through one of the top drawers. He made his way over to the center table clutching a small blue dish of pins. He set it on the table and moved the Episcopal chair with its bulky arms closer to where I was standing. He extended his palm, gesturing me to step on to the chair. Now I became really puzzled. I had expected him to give me the dish of pins and leave the tailoring to Richard. This was obviously not what he had in mind though. I looked at him for reassurance. I knew this chair to have a special significance. It was the Bishop's ritual to sit completely vested in it five minutes before mass and commit himself to prayer. Altar boys were not to sit in it let alone stand on it. He must have sensed my reluctance to violate this canon of propriety so to nudge me further he offered a thin smile and slight blinking of the eyes while nodding toward the chair.

There I was, looking down over the room while this holy man, a man of great stature in the church, served at my feet. It would have been odd enough to see him tailoring, but with him kneeling below, cloaked in the regalia of his calling, shook me to the core. Delicately, the aging pastor began to pin the bottom of my pant leg creating a make-shift hem. I became transfixed as the sharply pressed fabric of the rented pants mingled awkwardly with the embroidered edge on his silk sleeves while his hands worked. Looking displeased he said, "I don't think you will be satisfied with this. It balloons out too much at the bottom. It will look odd beside the rest of them." He glanced toward Richard's perfectly fitting pants. "I think we need to have a different strategy here."

'He said WE'?

The Bishop, gripping the thick arm of the chair, strained to get up. His knees cracked with the effort. He offered a breathless, "Let's see here." He began to bundle the extra material of the pant leg up under the jacket so that it bunched around my hip, thereby raising the bottom of the pant leg to its intended height without altering the cuff. "If we do it this way, the cuff will still be visible and you won't look any different than the others. Your jacket will hide where I pin. Take it off and we'll try it," he instructed. I complied, handing him the jacket while trying to push out some sort of acknowledgment of his suggestion. The words never came. I just smiled benignly.

Thoughts swirled. My mind took me to the many prayers professed here in this holy man's presence—masses, funerals and other sacraments. Even confession. They were Latin of course. If pressed I believe I could still recite a few of them, although when stopped in the middle of one, I'd surely have to start at the beginning to continue. Back then, when I used to pray, the words just tumbled out compliantly in a mindless thrumming mantra. *What kind of God would accept such a false rendering of devotion?* I'm taken by surprise at the boldness of this new thought but then, just as suddenly, feel ashamed for thinking it—unsettled by the hypocrisy of it all. After all, here I am, patching together my disguise, shamelessly campaigning for the lost blessings of a spent youth, preening before a god I had long since abandoned. *False? What truth is being told here?* Something is gnawing at the crust of who I think I am and I can't seem to swat it away.

The Bishop continued to implement the new strategy, stepping back periodically to see how things were lining up. Apparently pleased with what he saw, he pinned away until the job was completed. "Hmmm. I think that should do it. Put on the jacket and step down." He held out his hand to assist me. I did not need the help but took it nonetheless—the flesh-on-flesh moment eliciting strange synapses. There was an unexpected warmth to his touch. He ushered me over to the long mirror. There I stood, preening like a fashion model with the Bishop standing behind. My eyes focused on the flare of the jacket bulging slightly from the material tucked under it. My hips had widened noticeably making me look as if I was wearing an adult diaper. It wasn't great but it would do. Then I examined the cuff. It draped as it should, just over the shoe. I looked up to convey my satisfaction. Our mirrored faces locked. The Bishop offered only a perfunctory nod. He then turned, collected his prayer book from the bureau and walked out of the Sacristy into the hallway without a word. While his footsteps slowly faded, I glanced toward the door that led to the altar where the ceremony would soon begin. My eyes took me to the place where I would kneel in reverent supplication—my ill-fitting suit noticeable to only those who knew. *Reverent for the day* I thought, *just the day*.

When Quinn Was Not Himself

Honestly Quinn. You're like a turd stuck in a toilet bowl...always needing that second flush. Quinn smirked as he recalled Helen's remark while checking his side-view mirror. She could be comically crude like that when making a point, but he knew she was right. He was hesitant about going...even afraid. He needed a nudge and Helen knew him well enough to do the nudging. And here he was. The weather wasn't helping. The relentless slap of the windshield wipers added to his apprehensiveness as he peered through the wet darkness. Four miles of winding rural road and he couldn't find what he was looking for. The picture on the front of the soggy brochure laying on the passenger's seat showed an old farmhouse. It had been converted into an art gallery, named in honor of the famous landscape painter, Homer Watson.

But I don't know anything about painting, he remembered thinking as Helen presented him with a spanking new water-color paint kit. An envelope was tucked under a bright pink bow.

"Sorry about the bow," she winced. "It's all I had," hunching her shoulders in feigned defeat.

"Gee. Thanks. But my fortieth was twwwooo weeks ago?"

Helen flashed the brochure she was hiding behind her back and thrust it close to his face. "I know...jus found this the other day!"

"Oh. I see." He returned his attention to the gift. The bow did little to hide the wooden box the kit came in. A green label was stuck to the side, oddly drab for the creative intent of the box's contents. The words *Intermediate Water Color Kit* caught his attention along with a bulleted list of what was in the box: an easel, an array of paints, brushes, a plastic pallet, and what was termed, a *Getting Started Guide*. Quinn guessed from the apparatus attached to the back that it somehow transformed into an easel. He pondered the words *Assembly Required*. A shudder travelled through him recalling the frequent Christmases and birthdays that were spoiled while he grappled unsuccessfully with gifts that came with that same phrase.

"Open the card!" Helen demanded with playful annoyance.

"What's this? A used card?" That same card had previously come with a birthday gift: a coffin-shaped present containing among other things prune juice, anti-aging cream and a phony coupon for bulk orders of *Depends*. Helen enjoyed irreverent humor and with Quinn turning forty she had a convenient victim.

"I'm recycling! I thought you'd be proud of me... Mr. SCROOGE."

Quinn opened it while Helen looked on eagerly. In it was a folded paper, an invoice for a *Painter's Workshop*. On the bottom was a blue stamp marked PAID IN FULL and a hand-written note *With thanks, Marge, Gallery Hostess*. Quinn's eyes opened wide! "Two hundred and seventy-five dollars! That's a lot of money for an art lesson isn't it?"

Helen anticipated his reaction. "No. Look here," pointing to the brochure. "See. It's not just a lesson...it's a WHOLE WEEKEND WORKSHOP... one night and two days-worth of lessons! And it is with a PROFESSIONAL PAINTER!" Continuing in infomercial-mode she pointed while she read. "See ...instructions by famed water-color artist JACK REED!" She hoped this would be the clincher. It wasn't. He tried not to let on. Quinn perseverated on the word *famed*. He never felt as confident about his artistic talent as Helen did. She would often gush over the little doodles and sketches he would draw. He enjoyed hearing her accolades but at the same time felt falsely proud knowing she was not qualified to judge his amateurish work.

Quinn wondered what signals he may have conveyed to her to set this plan in motion.

"Nice," he said limply. "I'll have to look him up." Quinn's mind raced ahead. An image emerged. He could see himself nested in amongst a group of keeners. He could sense their eyes on him while *The Great Master* critiqued his work—*this is a good 1st attempt Quinn...why don't you look at how so-and-so does it...I hope you brought lots of paper*—scalded by the reductive tone in this imagined voice.

Helen sensed his waning enthusiasm. "Anyway. It's not for a couple of weeks so you can think about it." As an after-thought she added, "I could probably get a refund." She said it in a way that made that particular option sound less attractive...riskier perhaps. The experience of fifteen years of marriage taught him to be wary of situations where choices were not really choices at all—trap doors mostly. The need to tread cautiously had become an instinctive reflex.

"No. No don't do that. I'll go. I'm just a little nervous that's all."

****

The two weeks went by rather quickly. He thought reviewing the *Getting Started Guide* would allay his anxiety before the big weekend, but he got caught up with some other tasks and couldn't get to it. He was however able to rehearse setting the easel up and down several times, anticipating that a clumsy effort might draw undue attention, marking him as a man who had no legitimacy as an aspiring painter. A sticky peg securing the third leg to the metal bracket seemed the only troublesome feature of the apparatus, but he felt with frequent use the peg would become more cooperative.

Now the first evening of the weekend workshop was upon him and there was no turning back. He arrived home late from the office, the pelting rain causing traffic to crawl. A note from Helen greeted him on the kitchen counter. *I had to leave for my book club meeting...dinner plate is in the fridge...enjoy the workshop my little Rembrandt.* Then a smiley face. Unfortunately, the attempt at levity was lost on him. He felt harried as he often did in circumstances such as these. Prepared is what he would have preferred to feel...not rushed. He gulped his dinner, grabbed his materials and scurried out the door in a great haste.

The rain was not letting up. Fall leaves were everywhere and the strong wind pushed them sideways, tumbling in a furious dance in front of the car's lights. He checked his rear-view mirror as he was going quite slowly. He might have driven right past the entrance at least a couple of times. He couldn't be sure. Finally, his lights caught the image of two field-stone columns splotched with moss and dappled with wet lichen. The sturdy stonework supported a large rusted iron gate held open by a solitary rock. *This must be it* he thought, his spirits lifting. Turning into the driveway he could see a small metal sign identifying the building as *Homer Watson Gallery*. It was a sign well suited for the age of the building but unfortunately hopeless to those trying to find the place on a dark squalid night. Muted lights of the old farmhouse beckoned beyond the darkness. The shimmer of his headlights on the wetness of the many parked cars announced to him that he was among the last to arrive. He glanced at his watch. *Five after seven. Oh well. Five minutes late isn't bad*, he thought. The brochure said that refreshments and introductions would begin at 6:30. The lesson would start at 7:00 sharp. He would have liked the opportunity to meet a few of the other participants first so that he could explain his newness to this hobby. *As if they won't know* he chuckled to himself. He parked the car off to the side by a small barn-shaped building. He reached for the manila envelope that contained his registration materials. He fumbled through it for his name tag. *Might as well put it on now before I forget.* "Damn it! I thought I put it in here." He retraced his steps and remembered pinning it on to the painter's smock Helen bought him for the big weekend. "The painter's smock! You stupid idiot, you even forgot that!" castigating himself for his forgetfulness. *Maybe they will have a spare one,* he hoped. Anyway, there was nothing he could do now.

Bracing to be accosted by the night air, he opened the car door. A gust of wind caught it and yanked him sideways, pulling him almost completely out of the car. In the few seconds it took for him to reach into the back to get his supplies he was drenched. He hunkered down in the neck of his coat, tucked everything he could close to his chest and shuffled up the porch steps. His appearance had a marked similarity to a turtle walking upright. An ornate screen door, well-worn from careful but persistent handling, stood in front of a thick wooden one that framed a large beveled-glass window. *This place must have been some house in its day* he pondered. He tried the handle, but it was locked. He peered in, his vision distorted by the prism-effect of the glass. The hallway was dimly lit. No one was about. Off to the side he saw a metal plate that encased a button. *Ah..a door bell!.* To his delight, a pleasant chime rang loud enough to be heard over the roar of the wind and complaints from the tired hinges of the screen door. A few seconds later, he saw a figure of a young woman ascending a set of steps leading up from the basement. With an effortful thrust she opened the big door. That's when it all went terribly wrong for Quinn!

*****

In the room below the main gallery, Lindsey had just hung up the phone. It was Marge. Marge had called at around six o'clock to let Lindsey know that she felt ill and could not fulfill her role as session-hostess for this weekend's workshop with Jack Reed. "Would you be comfortable filling in Lindsey?" Marge asked between spasms of coughing.

Lindsey tethered her delight. "Sure. Don't worry about a thing." Lindsey was elated that Marge couldn't make it, not that she wanted her to be sick though. Lindsey was a senior in high school and was interning at the art gallery, hoping to use this experience to eventually get her into *The Draper*, a local college of art. When she applied for her internship experience at the Gallery, she had hoped she would be doing more 'artsy' type things instead of making coffee and serving baked goods. Marge, a middle-aged woman, had held the position of *Session Hostess* and coveted her role like a squirrel with a prized nut. When Lindsey came on board she made sure, in cleverly disguised ways, that Lindsey knew she was to be a subordinate and would remain as such. The Session Hostess was to ensure the guest instructors were introduced properly and made to feel welcomed. Over the years Marge had perfected the preparation necessary for this function and nothing was left to chance.

"I hope you feel better soon." Lindsey hung up. A broad smile erupted on her pretty face while she contemplated what she must do. She was cautiously confident she could handle things but she knew she would have to be extra attentive to the details. *Be professional Lindsey*, recalling her guidance counselor's remark to her last semester about being a bit too casual to be taken seriously.

Lindsey fished around the drawer and found the old label-maker. Smiling, she punched out the letters L-I-N-D-S-E-Y on the semi-rigid plastic tape. She cut it off at the right length, just enough to cover up the word MARGE on the session hostess' badge. After sticking it on she held the badge against the gold blazer Marge usually wore. There it was, Homer Watson Gallery Session Hostess with a small HWG logo on the top and Lindsey's name appropriately displayed below. She thought the colors coordinated nicely. She pinned it to the blazer pocket and then put it on. After modeling it in front of the mirror at a few different angles to make sure it looked just right, she giggled, admiring the transformation that had taken place. She felt a surge of importance as she viewed herself. This was her chance to shine.

Where did Marge say the biographical notes were for Jack Reed? she asked herself. *Ah, the recipe box.* She pulled out the small grey metal box that held index cards. There was an alphabetic indexing system that Marge used to file biographical information on guest instructors. Lindsey quickly went to 'R' and found the right card. The card was full of important details about the artist's accomplishments. She began reading the information aloud as a kind of rehearsal for what she would say later. *Wow! This guy must be pretty successful. He has paintings in Buckingham Palace!* She desperately wanted the participants to think how mature she was, how professional she was, how gracious she was but mostly she wanted the esteemed guest to notice her talent. Maybe she would even get a chance to show him some of her art work. *Wouldn't that be cool* she thought. A letter from a famous artist would be an excellent addition to her portfolio for *The Draper*. She had a strong feeling this was her moment. She placed the card in the blazer pocket.

It was getting close to six thirty. Lindsey double-checked the refreshment table to make sure everything was ready. The Gallery always provided guest artists with a complementary painter's smock embroidered with the HWG logo. She went to the locker where these were kept and to her surprise she found one with a Jack Reed name-tag already pinned on it. *Marge must have done this before she left last night* she thought. She pulled it off the hanger and hung it over the back of a chair close to where he would be working. She surveyed the room to make sure she hadn't forgotten anything. *Details. Remember the details Lindsey.* The chime of the doorbell interrupted her focus. She checked herself once more in the mirror and feeling satisfied went upstairs to welcome the distinguished guest artist and the other participants. When she got to the door, she could see a few people peering through the window. Their faces were distorted behind the ornate beveled glass.

"Hi. Welcome to the Homer Watson Gallery," she said in her most welcoming voice. "Sorry for keeping you out in the weather. We have to keep the door locked in the evening because the Gallery is closed," she explained to the first few people through the door. She was disappointed to see that they were all women. She was excited to introduce herself to Jack Reed and was hoping he would be among them. "There is a list on the table. Please check your name off so that I know who has arrived. We'll be setting up down stairs in the studio. You can take your wet things off and hang them in the closet down there. Help yourself to the refreshments and don't forget your nametags." She was shocked to hear herself articulate the instructions with such an *in-charge* voice. She adjusted her blazer and straightened her hostess badge. She judged from the reciprocal pleasantries offered to her that the people were comfortable with her and willing to accept her directions. This added to her burgeoning confidence.

"Awful weather out there isn't it?" she commented to the next few guests who arrived. She gave them the same directions as the other group. A glance at her watch told her it was six forty-five. *No Jack Reed. He is probably held up because of the weather* she thought. *He is coming from Bradford where ever that is.* Since she hadn't heard of it before, she figured it was at least a few hours away. A few more guests arrived. She checked the participant roster. Twelve of the thirteen expected guests were accounted for. Still missing was a Quinn Saunders. *Hmm...this will be the second Quinn I've run into* Lindsey thought while thinking about Quinn O'Keefe, a girl in her art history class. She liked the name Quinn. It sounded crisp and clean—much more definite than limp old Lindsey. Now it was seven. *Still no Jack Reed. I better go downstairs and explain to them that he had not arrived yet and it was probably due to the weather and the fact that he was coming from a long way.* This would be disappointing news, so she rehearsed her message. She felt it needs softening ...lessening the anxiety. She tried to anticipate their questions. *What if he doesn't show up? Would there be a refund?* She was delighted at her ability to attend to the details. Brimming with self-assurance she headed to the studio.

As she descended the stairs, she overheard three ladies talking. "This is my second workshop with him," a woman with a paint-stained smock said.

"Oh! I heard he was quite good," said another woman while setting up her easel. "This is my first serious lesson. I hope he is gentle," she giggled. "I'm a little nervous."

"I wouldn't say he was gentle. On the contrary, I think you will find him quite demanding," replied the woman. "He's kind of abrupt. Not that he's rude. He just tells you what he thinks of your work whether it's good or bad. You have to get used to him." Sensing the other woman's apprehension, she added. "I'm sure you'll be alright dear."

Lindsey liked what she was hearing. *He probably has a reputation for perfection...a letter from him on her application would surely be hard to ignore.*

Lindsey nervously provided the group with an update. She was a bit dejected that no one asked questions so to fill the time she took a short poll on who was familiar with Jack Reed's work and who wasn't. It turned out that about half the group knew of the painter and a few of them even had lessons from him before. The remainder knew nothing more than what they had read in the brochure. Some informal chatting started after Lindsey's poll. Lindsey waited, glancing at her watch periodically. She began to wonder what she would do if he actually didn't show up. The thought made her more nervous, so she stopped thinking about it and tried to follow a few of the conversations that were going on. Finally, the chime rang. Lindsey checked her watch. *Five after seven. Not too bad* she thought. "That must be him!" she blurted. She censured her enthusiasm almost immediately. *Be professional Lindsey* she reminded herself. Adopting a more moderate tone she added, "I'll be right back." She checked her blazer pocket for the biographical information and straightened her badge and went up the stairs to greet the special guest.

As she walked down the hallway she could see a man peeking through the window. She was instantly relieved. Curiously though, the man on the other side of the door looked a bit younger than what she was expecting. After reading Jack Reed's biography on Marge's notes she anticipated an older man, perhaps in his sixties. *Maybe he just looks younger* she thought. *Better make sure Lindsey.* As she opened the door, a great gust of wind thrust the screen door out of the man's hand. In his attempt to regain his grip on it, he dropped the box he was holding causing quite a clamor. At precisely that same moment Lindsey posed this seemingly innocuous question. "Jack Reed?"

With the din from the howling wind in his face, the screen door threatening to fly from his hand, the calamity of dropping his materials, and all of this coupled with his manifest insecurity from not only being a *green horn* but also quite late, Quinn made what would become a disastrously faulty assumption about what the young woman had asked. Quinn was known for his annoying tendency to see ambiguity where others didn't, and this characteristic made conversation with him more of a chore than it should have been. *Too many questions! What part of this do you not understand?* Helen would playfully jibe. He knew this of himself of course and was bothered enough to be at least semi-committed to changing this unfortunate trait. A clear-headed self-assurance is how he would have preferred to be perceived—someone who could take it all in very quickly and not toil needlessly with *did she mean this* or *did she mean that?* Resolute...that's how he wanted to be thought of by others. So, without his usual trepidation he made an instantaneous, but irretrievably fateful inference. She had asked *Jack Reed?* as if she were asking *Are you here for Jack Reed's workshop.* After all he was late, and Jack Reed had no doubt started so what else could she have meant? Thus, nudged by his circumstances—on his knees, dripping wet, grasping on to a rebellious door with one hand while trying to collect the spilled contents of his kit with the other—he didn't bother asking her to clarify her question. To do so would surely announce himself to this eager young woman that he was someone who needed things explained much more fully... a remedial learner perhaps. No. He would not ask her what she meant. He didn't have to. *Helen would be so pleased.* Thus, to the question she posed, *Jack Reed?,* he unequivocally answered, "Yes," with as much conviction as he was capable of mustering.

"Good. I'm so pleased you found the place," she said pleasantly. "My name is Lindsey. I'm the session-hostess." *Don't talk too much Lindsey* she said to herself. *He is not interested in you right now...he's probably concerned about being late.* "Let me help you with your things. We're downstairs...everyone is anxious to get started." Lindsey was delighted by her professionalism. Images of Marge's subdued displeasure at hearing how well she was able to rise to the occasion bubbled through her.

Quinn dwelled on her comment that they were waiting for him to arrive. *Shit. I'm holding everyone up. Just what I needed.* He gathered the rest of his things while she kept the screen door from blowing off its hinges. When safely in, Lindsey asked him if there was anything that she could do for him to help him get ready. "Thanks. That's kind of you. Uhm... actually...I left my smock at home. Would you happen to have a spare one?"

Lindsey paused for a moment as if puzzled by his question. "Yes. Yes of course," she offered cautiously. "We have one downstairs for you...complements of the gallery."

"Oh? I thought I was to bring my own," he said meekly, too meekly to be heard.

Lindsey began to lead Quinn down the hallway toward the stairs that would take them to the studio. "Oh Miss. One other thing. I...I also forgot my name tag. Will that be a problem?"

Lindsey paused again before answering. *Artists are weird* she thought. "Not at all. We have one made up for you already."

This was really confusing Quinn. He was sure he was to bring these things. The registration materials that were sent to his home clearly stated the additional requirements. *Maybe Helen can return the smock and get a refund. I won't need two* he thought.

Lindsey led Quinn down a narrow staircase at the back of the old house. He was expecting to smell the must of damp stone as he descended but the walls of the foundation had been painted a bright white and there wasn't a hint of dampness. He was also expecting to hear Jack Reed's voice addressing the group but all he heard was casual chatting. Two flights and then a small set of steps to the left led him into the studio. The room was awash with light. *That's good* he thought. *Artists need lots of good lighting.* As his eyes adjusted to the brightness he saw that everyone had their easels set up and paints in order. *Oh great! Now I am going to be on display while they watch me fumble with my stuff.* He looked around the room for a space to park himself. Being an old basement there were a lot of nooks and crannies. He spotted a small open space toward the back of the studio. *That'll be perfect* he thought. He anxiously looked to Lindsey for her approval. To his disappointment, she motioned him to another spot, one that was far more conspicuous than he had hoped. *Where is the instructor going to sit?* he thought while moving to the spot she had indicated. He began by putting his equipment down, so he could take off his coat and commence with the ordeal of unpacking his kit. As he did so he felt a bit peculiar. It seemed that all the people in the room were women and he couldn't see Jack Reed anywhere. Quinn looked on either side of where he was setting up. *Could it be that he isn't here yet?* he mused. This was good news. Quinn opened his kit and began the set-up routine that he had rehearsed at home. *I hope the peg holds* he wished.

"When you are ready, your smock is on the chair," Lindsey nodded to the forest green smock close to where Quinn was assembling his materials. He smiled affirmatively and glanced quickly to the chair she was referring. He thought it odd that the smock was a different color than what the others were wearing. Cleaner too. He returned his attention to his easel. *Damn it. This peg is going to give me trouble again* thinking about how it gave way at home a few times. He would have to make do. *There. That should hold it* he thought, willing the peg to perform its intended function. *I better get my smock on before I set up the paints.* Quinn moved over to the chair where Lindsey had placed the smock. He was anxious to get back to set up his paints before the instructor arrived. The smock was draped on the chair with the name tag concealed in one of the folds. In Quinn's haste to get it on, it did not occur to him to look at it.

Lindsey, seeing Quinn don his smock, took that as her cue and pulled the card containing the biographical information from her blazer pocket. She cleared her throat providing a subtle signal to the group that she was about to announce something. Up to this point, the women in the room had been chatting with one another. After a polite pause, conversations gradually ceased. Quinn wasn't sure what Lindsey was going to say but he knew it would be rude to continue fussing with his paints, so he stopped what he was doing and looked across the room at his fellow participants. Lindsey began reading from a card. While the participants listened, Quinn noticed that the expression on their faces were oddly varied. Some smiled with anticipatory delight while others had a different expression. Rather, they looked on with puzzled suspicion as one might expect of an audience in a magic show, waiting to see if they could detect the slight-of-hand that the magician was skillfully keeping from view. Lindsey was about halfway through her introduction when Quinn made a more earnest attempt to attend to what the cheery young assistant was saying. *Was she introducing Jack Reed?* Quinn scanned the room nervously. He was still the only male. *That's odd* he thought. *Where do they keep him?*

"Please join me in welcoming Jack Reed." Lindsey had delivered her biographical introduction flawlessly. Brimming with pride, she placed her card back in her blazer pocket and began to applaud while turning to offer Quinn her most charming smile. That's when the penny dropped. Quinn's comfort level plummeted. Gripped by a tight-sphinctered sensation he nervously looked out into the room. Bright happy faces contrasted sharply with facial contortions the likes of which he hadn't seen before. *Have I just been introduced as Jack Reed?* He shot a desperate glance at Lindsey. She was so happy, so official looking with her gold blazer and her glorious session-hostess badge. How would he tell her?

"No! No I mean...there's been a mistake. I...I'm not Jack Reed." There was a prolonged pause. Suddenly Lindsey's expression was transformed from a brimming pride to astonished incredulity, and finally to a tearful, red-faced embarrassment. "I'm Quinn Saunders!" he shouted desperately while holding up his name tag for all to see. Quinn hoped that the name tag would reorient the poor girl. This didn't seem to help. Quinn glanced down at the name tag he was so vigorously using as his defense. There it was, *Jack Reed*. Tragically, it all made sense to him now.

Unable to subdue her anger, Lindsey protested, "But...you said you WERE Jack Reed!" She began to sob inconsolably.

"Yes...but I thought you meant..." Quinn's voice faded, unable to muster enough ardor to persuade the troubled throng that he was not the perpetrator they thought he was. Lindsey was really crying now. Her nose glistened like a glazed doughnut. Someone handed her a rag from their paint supplies. That brought on more tears and even louder sobs. The image of this bright effervescent young woman convulsed in tears, apparently at the hands of this callous trickster, would not go away with a simple explanation. Vicious stares silently admonished him for his role in this evil-doing. If there was anyone in the room who might have entertained the slightest possibility that there could have been an understandable mistake here, it was not evident to him. He thought it wiser to keep quiet.

To suggest that the remainder of the evening was an uncomfortable one for Quinn Saunders would have been a gross understatement. The real Jack Reed did arrive eventually. The chime rang a few moments after Quinn's ill-fated attempt to explain how his identity got lost in the interpretation of Lindsey's initial question. Lindsey, feeling far too vulnerable now, could not go up to greet him as she had hoped she would be able to do. Instead she ran to the restroom. A take-charge type of woman went in her place. Quinn sat paralyzed, caught in a trance trying to reconstruct the evening in his mind, desperate to find a way he could turn back time to have it end more positively. When Jack Reed entered the studio the woman who escorted him must have told him about the problem because he directed his first gaze right at Quinn. Coming slowly to the awareness that he still had on the artist's smock, name tag and all, he unceremoniously disrobed in front of the group in a pathetic gesture of defeat and handed it to the famous painter. Jack Reed, a humorless man, grunted his disapproval and placed the smock on a dusty table holding it as if it had been dipped in sheep excrement. Quinn offered no explanation. A woman who had had lessons from the painter in the past gave an impromptu introduction to their esteemed guest while Lindsey's wails could be heard in the background. In the middle of the subdued applause, Quinn's easel collapsed with a clamor, the fouled peg the culprit. Quinn, knelt to repair it but changed his mind mid-way, frozen in place by an icy stare from the great artist.

Quinn didn't learn much about painting that evening. Nor did he return for the Saturday, or the Sunday for that matter. Cheap as he was, he didn't trouble Helen to obtain a refund.

News From Meaford

"This is not a good idea Bill," he remembered his wife saying. She was right and he knew it but a compulsion had taken over him. Now here he was, three thousand feet in the air, floating over a featureless landscape, heading to a lake that wasn't even named. His mind was on rewind looping back to that day when he pitched his plan to her. She was angry about it, the kind of anger born of frustration. "Besides," she argued. "you don't even know if he is going to be there for GOD SAKES,...even worse, he may not want to see you! Have you even thought of that?" Her eyes were white-hot. "Oh what's the use in talking. Honestly Bill, I don't know who you are anymore!" She had always thought of him as being so rational, a successful businessman who took pride in managing risks. And now this impulsiveness! "Oh go do what you want. You are going to do it anyways, I can see that." She turned her back on Bill and looked out the kitchen window at her garden. "Just have to tell Dr. Patel you ignored her advice I guess."

He tried to reason with her. "Dr. Patel said it would be *risky* Ann, not deadly. AND, she's the one who encouraged me to find him in the first place! Remember?"

"Find him yes, not GO GET HIM!"

Bill was a hopeless tangle of emotions since that day at the doctor's office. He couldn't seem to get Teddy out of his mind. He ended with a feeble plea, "Please Ann. Try and understand. It's something I just have to do."

Clint's excited voice pulled him back from his trance. "There's the place!"

Bill turned abruptly and squinted into the sun. "Where?" he asked straining to see over the instruments. "I don't see anything."

"There. See the smoke," Clint shouted over the steady roar of the single-engine Piper. "That's O'Rourke's cabin!" Bill was stunned by the certainty in Clint's voice. There was no 'maybe' or 'I think'. 'That's

O'Rourke's cabin'. His plan suddenly went from tenuous to tangible in an instant, and with it, a tumult of angst.

As they got closer, Clint banked the plane into a turn allowing a better view. He glanced at Bill confirming he was looking in the right spot. Bill gave him a voiceless smile, surrendering to the staccato hammering of the plane's angry pistons. A small clearing at the north end of the lake came into view. Smoke ebbed from the chimney of the larger of two buildings and a smoldering fire burned unattended closer to the second one. Bill saw movement in amongst the trees. *He must be down there* he thought.

"I'll take her down into the wind and taxi back," Clint yelled over the roar.

Stumps from severed trees dotted the perimeter of the clearing. Ribbons of well-trampled footpaths led here and there conveying a bustling hive of chore work. A jagged peninsula jutted out from the shore providing a refuge from the sweep of open water. Further up silvery flecks from a bubbling creek danced in the sun while it spilled velvety swirls into the lake. The creek connected to an expansive network of ponds dammed by an industrious beaver. And to the north, a navigable river snaked lazily off into the distance. The tranquility of it all belied the grim purpose for Bill's visit.

There was a small beach area. Two canoes and an over-turned wooden boat, its once-red bottom scarred with wear, lay idle on the muddy shore. A crude dock angled out. Bill could see it was narrow, ruptured in spots, heaved from the grip of winter-ice. Its slats were unevenly spaced like the broken keyboard of a thrift store piano.

Clint circled expertly and began his approach to the water. There were a few mild lurches as the pontoons kissed the top of the waves. As he eased the drive out of the propeller the plane sagged, then leveled off compliantly. With its forward motion subsiding talking became easier.

"I'm not sure how long I'm going to be," Bill said. "Can you wait off shore? I don't want the plane to be a distraction."

Clint pondered this for a moment. "Sure?" he said hesitantly. "You got me for the day. Take as long as you need. It's your nickel. There's an island at the other end of the lake. I'll tie up there, out of the wind." With that he reached under his seat and pulled out a dusty fishing tackle box. "Here. Take these." He handed Bill a plastic hand gun and two cartridges that looked like fire crackers. He could see the alarm in Bill's face. "It's a flare gun...easy peezy. Just put the flare in the slot, aim up in the air toward the middle of the lake and then pull the trigger. It'll boom in the air and then flare for a minute or two. I'll come when I hear it."

Bill fumbled with it in his hand for moment, taking in its mechanism. It seemed simple enough. "Why two?" he asked.

Clint considered the question briefly and then offered a wry grin and a mischievous wink. "If you shoot the second one, I'll come a bit faster." His dark humor did little to quell Bill's anxiousness. He gave Clint an obliging smile and tucked the gun with the cartridges into his sack.

As the plane drifted toward the dock a wolf-sized dog and a couple of children bounded down to the shore stopping at the water's edge. Their ink-black hair and bronze skin confirmed it. *They were Dene alright* he thought. A moment later a woman and an older girl emerged from behind the cabin. He had been told by the investigator he had hired that Teddy was living with an indigenous woman and her three children. He thought he had processed this already but the reality of it snuck up on him. He wasn't as ready for this as he thought. In his mind's eye it was just he and Teddy, not with someone else's wife and someone else's children. His mission seemed messier somehow. Then a man appeared in the cabin doorway. *That's Teddy* he thought. *It's him! It's finally him!*

Clint brought the plane perpendicularly to the front of the dock before killing the engine. "Okay," Bill said. "This is it. Could be five minutes or five hours." Clint shrugged his acknowledgement of Bill's circumstances and he opened the flimsy door. The crisp coolness of the fall air reminded him of how far north he had come. He made a clumsy exit on to the pontoon cautiously navigating the irregularities of the plane's geometry.

"Will he bite?" Bill shouted—the curled-lip snarl of the dog arresting his progress.

Teddy's expression didn't change. He continued to stare while the dog menaced him from shore. The moment froze in an inhospitable state. This wasn't how he imagined it would go. Then, as if a mandatory threshold of time had elapsed, Teddy gave a subtle whistle with his teeth. Instantly the dog ceased his aggression and flanked back toward him and lay at his feet, whimpering and wagging his welcome with the enthusiasm of a small puppy. Still, not a word was spoken.

"You may not believe this but it's me, Bill...your brother." The words felt hollow. He regretted how they tumbled out.

Teddy raised his eyebrows and drew his head back. He turned and looked at the woman. She shot back an apprehensive stare. He shrugged and looked back at his visitor. "Billy?" he questioned. "That you?"

"It's me alright."

"Bin a'while." The flatness in his voice was unsettling.

"Quite a while I'd say...forty three years to be exact." Bill let the words settle. "Too long, way too long."

Teddy yanked his head to the side gesturing him to come on shore. Turning, Bill gave a thumbs up to Clint. He fired up the Piper and headed up the lake.

Bill stumbled with the unevenness of the dock, poking and prodding each successive slat with his feet. There was a spring in the log-span and it tilted perilously to one side forcing his eyes to be welded to the task of staying upright. He inched along not daring to look up. There was no 'be careful' or 'watch your step' as Teddy watched from shore. An intruder. That's what he felt like.

Once on shore, they stood face to face, mining each other's features, looking for anything that would bind them as brothers—any tells from their shared heritage lingering in the creviced folds of their once-younger faces. He looked grizzled, not a full beard, more of a scissor-shave. There were blank spots on his left side—skin grafts from the burns he encountered in the fire. Whiskers wouldn't grow there. That, and his icy blue eyes. Bill knew it was him.

"Well?" Bill wanted him to take the lead. Instead, they stood suspended in awkwardness. Eventually he put up his arms and stepped forward beckoning a hug but Teddy made no reciprocal gesture. An impenetrable void persisted. Tears pooled up in his eyes and his words got clogged in thick emotion.

Teddy stepped back to examine the visitor. "I see it's you right enough. How the hell...Billy? Why'd you come...." His eyes bored through him.

––––––––––

Bill's arrival must have taken them from their chores. There was evidence of preparation everywhere. Fresh skins were drying in the sun. A branch cut head-high held a variety of rusted metal traps clanging in the wind. A monstrous stack of firewood walled up between two trees explained the piles of sawdust and woodchips scattered about. A modest garden looked picked over. Stunted corn stocks and the leafy tops of root vegetables lay wrinkling in the waning sun. Whatever harvest they were expecting was already in and from the size of the garden, it couldn't have been much. Everything spoke to the precariousness of eking out an existence here—the effort, the perils, all relentlessly gnawing away at their ankles. One wondered what refuge this place offered—why and was it worth it?

The cabin was Spartan. It was a single room with a curtained corner strung with a clothesline cordoning off a sleeping area. A sooty wood stove stood proudly in the center. It was maimed with a damaged leg.

A large rock served adequately as a make-shift crutch. Still, it gave off a comforting heat making the place almost pleasant. The interior side of the logs were hued a rustic patina, black in spots. There was a sheen to them—vestiges of grease-laden steam emanating from years of ventless cooking no doubt. Iron pots hung from pegs cleverly inserted into well positioned slots. A porcelain table, chipped and dinted, was likely used as both an eating table and a food preparation counter. Although there were five in the family, only two rickety wooden chairs could be seen, one mended with binder twine and tree sap. Teddy blew dust from a blackened kettle, ladled some water from a bucket and placed it on the stove. He spooned in some tea and pulled up a chair.

There they sat, sipping tea and talking while his family returned to their chores. The conversation was clumsy, maze-like—a lot of starting and stopping. "Remember the last time I saw you?" Bill asked. Teddy shook his head. "It was in front of Dempsey's Hardware ...remember Dempsey's?" Teddy nodded. "You would've been about nine at the time. I was with my Dad." Teddy cocked his chin to the side. His gaze intensified. Bill continued. "You were just getting into the van as I recall...with some kids...what was the name of that place you..."

"Beacon House," he blurted. "It was called Beacon House." His words rolled out slowly, his forehead pinched tight. There was a long pause. "Dad? Wud'ya mean Dad?" Teddy asked. Bill had trespassed on a twitchy emotion.

Bill considered his question, cautious about Teddy's tone. He didn't know what Teddy could remember—what he wanted to forget. "After the fire ...I was adopted...the Clarkes adopted me. You knew that right?"

"You called him 'Dad'?"—spoken less as a question, more of a condemnation. Bill had never processed this with his brother. He never had the chance, at least that's what he told himself.

"Yeah. I called him 'Dad'," Bill admitted. He waited a minute trying to discern the impact the conversation was having. He wanted to move on...get to the point of why he was there but had stumbled into unexplored terrain. "I heard that it didn't go that well for you at Beacon. You ran away a few times? That right?" Teddy gave no response. Billy nudged some more. "Dad and Mom...the Clarkes...they got updates from the social worker...said you were dealing with a lot of trauma?" He looked for affirmation from Teddy but none came. "Found out later you were fostered out to a group home in Orangeville." Teddy took a sip of tea and stared at Bill blankly. He continued, "...must'a bin pretty awful for you."

Teddy glanced over his shoulder toward the window. "Not so bad...didn't bother me much."

Bill felt he had slipped down a rabbit hole and was having trouble finding his way back. He was hoping Teddy would be more forthcoming—open up about why he wanted to escape. He didn't. Bill continued to pursue it. "You think about that much...I mean the fire? You know, how it started...that kind'a thing?"

Staring at the floor Teddy replied, "Dad." He looked up, his expression cold and blank. "They told me Dad started it...just before he killed himself."

Bill's eyes grew. "So you knew then?"

He nodded, his face unchanged. Bill was expecting rage, not apathy. Was it hidden, out of reach perhaps, or simply not there? Something was clearly stuck in Teddy's psyche and Bill's prodding wasn't going to pry it loose. He decided to change the subject. "How did it go for you in Orangeville? Was it a good place?"

Teddy looked past him like a department store manikin, "Very religious..." he murmured, his smile thin and haunting.

"Oh?...didn't know that. They treat you okay there?" Bill wondered why he asked the question.

Teddy gave an indifferent snort. "Hmm. Like I said, they were religious." The moment hung in the air like a miasmal stench. Nothing else was said...nothing need be said. Bill's mind raced in a thousand directions as they sat. He sensed his purpose slipping away. "Teddy. I have something to tell you." Teddy's eyes opened a bit wider. He cocked his head to one side and readied himself to listen. "I have been quite sick. I had a massive heart attack about a year and a half ago."

"Hmm?" Teddy responded.

Bill continued, "...had to sell my business...heart couldn't take the stress."

Teddy wrestled with the news, wondering how it fit. "Yer okay?"

"Yes. Yes I'm okay...okay until the next one that is."

"Next one?"

"The doctors said I have a heart defect...a problem with one of my valves. It got badly damaged when I had the attack. They did what they could but they couldn't repair it." Teddy nodded. It was the closest demonstration of empathy Bill would get from him. "They said it was genetic...my heart defect...you know, inherited...you get it from your parents." He paused to confirm he was being understood. "And, that's why I'm here."

They sat in silence, sipping tea. Eventually Teddy spoke. "You think I may have it too...the defect." This was not a question. He completely understood.

"That's right," Bill said, relieved for the clarity. "If they had known my valve was damaged they could have corrected it before my heart attack. Now it's too late for me but maybe not for you."

Teddy cocked his head to one side. "Wud'ya mean?"

"Well...maybe you could get checked out...you know...to see if you had the defect. If you do, they can fix it!" *Jesus Bill, you sound like you are selling a used car* he thought. Teddy stared at him for a moment, then got up from his chair and made his way to the window. He looked out at his family sawing and splitting wood. It was a prideful gaze, a kind of satisfaction in it. Bill continued. "Don't worry about expenses...I can get you there and back. I have the money...can stay with Ann and I until you're all mended up." He stopped to take stock.

Teddy's expression hadn't changed. "...can bring the family too if you want. We have lots of room," he added. He wasn't sure if he should have said this—how Ann would take it.

Teddy rubbed the stubble on his chin. "You say I might have this defect from our parents?" Bill nodded affirmatively. "Don't know which one though right?" Again he nodded wondering why this mattered. Teddy mulled this over for quite some time. It seemed an important distinction for him to make. "...might not too eh...have it that is?"

"Yes, I suppose, but they say there's a good chance. They say there is an eighty percent chance siblings ..." Teddy's expression prompted Bill to rephrase. "Most brothers or sisters inherit the same defect. Not everyone, but most do."

"That's what they say, is it?" The tinge of sarcasm prickled. Teddy turned and abruptly changed the subject. "You got'a new bike that day."

"Bike? What do you mean?"

"That day at Dempsey's...I called you over...member? You were try'n to stuff it into the trunk of that big Caddie."

"Oh?...that's right...yeah. I think it was my birthday or something...maybe my twelfth? Dad and I were...the Clarkes," he corrected. "...they bought me a bike that day."

"Ya didn't come over...jus waved."

"I uh...well uh..it was my birthday...had to go I guess."

"Saw your d-a-d point towards me. Ya shook your head...jus waved...didn't come over...didn't seem to want to."

Bill felt winded by his recollection, a real punch in the gut. He was paralyzed. The air was brittle with tension. A cascade of guilt poured over him. He was the older brother. *Did I let this happen?* he lamented. After the tragedy the boys were pulled apart...willingly for Bill...too willingly. It was as if the fire had cauterized that part of his life and blood no longer flowed from there. When the Clarkes adopted him, everything was pleasantly vanquished from his consciousness. No more alcoholic father spewing his rage. No more depressed mother, callused-over, unable to feel...numb to the needs of her children. And, Teddy. He could be looked after...someone else could do that...other than him. Relief! That is what he felt but he didn't know it. It just felt 'better'...much better and he didn't want to let go of the feeling. He'd go through the motions now and again. He'd ask about Teddy. That's what brothers are supposed to do, but in truth he didn't want to know. He didn't want bad news. 'No news is good news' they'd say...and it was.

Finally Teddy broke through it all. "Yer not here cuz'a my defect are ya?"

"Wud'ya mean?"

"Well, I think yer here for sumth'n else." Their eyes locked. Bill felt he'd been asked a question, one which Teddy knew the answer to. The ball was in his court. "Member that night Billy? Member where you were?"

"I uh...I was at the Palmer's ...at Robbie's...member Robbie Palmer?" Teddy waited. Bill felt compelled to provide more. "Yah,...had a big fight with Dad...he was roaring drunk...I ran out'a the house...mad as hell." More silence.

Teddy got up and opened the stove. He poked it a few times until a few sparks came to life and then he added another log. He had his back to Bill. He took his time before talking. "He locked me in our room Billy...fraid I was goin with you I guess...I used the window." His eyes misted up, "...too late for mom."

This was the festering canker he had hid from all these years. That fateful night Teddy had gone back into the house to try and save their mother and burned himself in the process. He wasn't there and he should have been. Instead he was hiding out with his friend Robbie Palmer in their back shed. The two of them were playing checkers by flashlight. "It's your turn," he recalled Robbie saying. Bill was distracted. "Hear that?" Bill asked. "Sirens!...Sounds close...must be a fire..." Bill returned to the game, "...my turn right?

———–

The winter passed in Meaford. It was a mild one as winters go. Ann and Bill were able to take a couple of weeks in Hawaii and now they were back waiting for the remaining clumps of snow to rot away. Bill's heart was still ticking although breathlessness and a perpetual ache in his legs had become more prevalent. Still he was alive. A letter came in the mail while they were gone. It was postmarked 'Hay River, N.W.T.'. There was no return address. It was from Clint, the pilot Bill hired to fly him into Teddy's lake. It wasn't much of a note, just a clipped out portion of a newspaper. It read,

> 'Reclusive trapper, Edward (Teddy) O'Rourke was found dead in the Kakisa Lake region. The cause of death appeared to be hypothermia. The RCMP feel he may have stumbled while tending his trap-line and became unconscious after hitting his head. His death has been ruled accidental. There is no known next of kin.'

No known next of kin. Bill kept repeating the phrase. *How could this be?* Tears dripped on to the clipping as he held it. Bill's mind swirled reaching for affirmation that something had been lost here, something worthy of the grief he felt. Emptiness...it was over. He went over to the drawer to place the clipping in with the scrapbook he had been preparing. Something rolled to the front as he opened it. There it was! He was sure he had misplaced it. It was the unused flare cartridge. It lay right on top of a well-creased black and white photo he had put aside. He and Teddy were standing next to each other while their mother was on the left, her hand on Bill's shoulder. On the right was Teddy. The photo had been cut with scissors and all that remained of the image that was severed was a single hand placed on Teddy's shoulder. Bill knew whose hand it was. *The picture looks almost normal* he thought.

He held the cartridge, rolling it between his fingers thinking about the day Clint gave it to him. *I only needed one... just the one.*

The Old Man Who Came Late

"Kelly. Can you get the lights?" The moderator paused. "The back ones too please." Kelly flicked the right-hand switch up and down a few times and then shrugged. "No? Oh well. I guess the front ones will have to do." A few coughs and the rustling of chairs could be heard as the audience adjusted their eyes to the new brightness. The moderator smoothed her skirt as she rose from her chair. She began her perfunctory message of appreciation. "I would like to thank Daniel Cote for submitting this very interesting film." Daniel produced a measured smile. The sporadic applause died down quickly. "We have a few moments before viewing the next one. Does anyone have any questions for Daniel?"

A clank from the back of the room caused a few to turn toward the old man who had come late. His cane had slipped and fell against the metal chair beside him. Grim-faced he wedged it between his seat and the vacant one next to him, emitting a slight grunt from the effort. The drip from his wet fedora pooled in front of him as he sat alone in the shadows shrouded by several rows of empty chairs. The brochure he had been given at the door was clutched firmly in his hand. A prominent smudge from the wetness of his thumb had obscured the film title he had come to see, *The Alias Dr. Haston.*

"What! No questions? I thought for sure there would be a flood of ques...oh good...there's one."

Daniel shuffled in his seat anticipating the young woman's question.

"I liked your film," she giggled. "I was like wondering, is he like still alive?"

Daniel stood to respond. He tugged at his ascot and gave a slight twist to his beret. "Well. Thanks for the question." He sat on the edge of the table and pulled up a chair to prop his leg on. It was important for him to eschew any tinge of formality. "My original intention was to find him but I was not able to track him down. It's been fifty years don't forget." He paused to let that sink in. "He'd be in his eighties if he were still alive! It's possible he is still out there somewhere but I checked...police records...missing persons...that kind of thing. Other aliases too." Heads nodded. "Nothing. I let the posting stay up for the full year! None of the folks who came forward with their stories knew of his whereabouts...just seem to vanish!" Many mumbled at this disclosure. Daniel continued. "Although I should tell you I got a curious email one day...right out of the blue ...just as I was wrapping up. I thought I was on to something." While shaking his head he added, "...turned out to be a dead-end though."

"Dead end?" queried the moderator. A few in the room murmured their agreement to the question.

"Well, I exchanged several emails with the writer. I actually thought it might have been 'HIM' at one point! He...or the writer I should say...seemed to have specific information about Haston that jived well with what I had learned about the story. I got excited! However, when I suggested a Skype call that's when all communication stopped." Shrugging his shoulders he lamented, "Figured it must have been a prank."

Excited chatter trickled through the room.

"Hmm...interesting." The moderator looked out at the audience. Are there any more questions for Daniel?"

A young man at the side of the room grabbed a microphone. "Yeah. I had heard about this guy from my grandparents when I was deciding to go to this University. They were here back then. Big scandal! I'm wondering what he was like in person...you know...what was he like to hang with...you know...did he like beer and stuff?" A few chuckles accompanied the young man as he took his seat.

Smiling, Daniel responded, "Well, at least I know what you value in your education." Laughter ensued. He continued joking. "There might be a few people in the room who encountered him around town back then. Let me see." Daniel surveilled the audience. "Anyone drink beer with Haston?" he shouted. Lots of good-natured chortling rumbled through the group. Assuming no one would be of that vintage, Daniel focused on some retired faculty he saw in the audience. "Ah! I recognize Professor Wilson, Conrad Wilson retired chair of the Psychology Department and yes, there's Pamela Nelson former secretary from the Dean's office. Can either of you answer the young man's question?"

Without waiting an eager attendant thrust a mic toward Professor Wilson. Emanating anoyance, he held the mic like a rancid sausage, "Well uh, I uh don't drink beer...although he may have." There was distain in his voice. "I suppose I considered him a colleague at that time, though I should add I was suspicious of him from the outset...something wasn't quite right. I detected a kind of shallowness in his thinking...tried to alert my colleagues but they wouldn't have it." He paused momentarily while ignoring his wife's gestural admonishment. "I seem to recall that Haston was working on something called *Attributional Ascriptions*...an interesting topic I suppose but I could see he did not have an adequate grasp of it... not something I felt rose to the level scholarship I was used to...certainly not tenure-worthy in my estimation." Wilson craned his arthritic neck to view the listeners better. People seemed to be talking. He glumly handed the mic back to the attendant. His eyes sagged with disappointment as he slumped back in his seat while his wife patted his hand.

Pamela Nelson held her hand up part way. With an affirmative nod from the moderator she made her way to the isle-mic. "Can you hear me? Good." She paused to collect her composure. "As the film pointed out, I was Dean Whitting's secretary." Half-turned, her eyes landed on the old man at the back. Something held her gaze for a brief moment as she tried to discern the shadowed features of the onlooker. The back of the room, half lit, tinted his glasses an opaque grey. His face looked hollowed out, corpse-like—an eyeless apparition peering out from the darkness. "As I was saying, I knew Dr. Haston from his visits to the office...meetings with the Dean and such...a pleasant man really...he was very kind for such a bright man." Professor Wilson stirred uncomfortably in his seat. She continued, "The students loved him. I collected the semester-end evaluations for the department and his were always very high...higher than the others in the Department!" she added. Dr. Wilson held his sour grimace. He rubbed his fingers incessantly while rustling in his seat.

A woman close to her didn't wait to get to a mic. "Did y'ever see them interact?" she shouted.

"Who? The Dean and Dr. Haston?" Ms. Nelson asked. The woman nodded. "Well yes...yes of course. Everything seemed quite okay with them if that's what you are hinting at. I think they were friendly. They joked with one another." She thought for a moment and then added, "Dr. Whitting liked to practice his French with Dr. Haston. He was bilingual you know!"

Daniel interjected. "Actually Haston knew several languages." The audience nodded appreciatively.

Ms. Nelson continued, "But when the story broke, that was different. Dean Whitting was quite disturbed by the whole thing as you might expect. I mean with a scandal like that...he would have felt responsible. He hired the man after all...checked his credentials...that type of thing." She began to tear-up. She choked out the next few sentences. "It devastated him! I was worried...I thought he might have another heart attack. The poor man had to take a medical leave shortly afterward." An impatient student shouted from the middle of the room, "Did you ever see Haston's credentials?"

Ms. Nelson, a bit miffed at the young man's lack of propriety, replied. "Well...yes. At one point I filed his paperwork for the Dean...you know...reports, vitae...that kind of thing. The faculty files were kept in the Deans office in those days." She paused for a moment as if trying to scrub out the possibility of scandal in what she was about to say. She began slowly, "Dr. Haston's file had been..."

"Please!" Professor Wilson shouted. "Can we stop calling him Dr. Haston! He was a fraud! An imposter!" There was an abrupt silence. Aware that his excesses may have betrayed his deep contempt for Haston he managed to apprehend his fury and return to a more reasoned tone. "We shouldn't forget this man would have been in jail had he been caught."

"I am sorry Dr. Wilson. It's just...it's just that it's all I knew him as." Ms. Nelson continued. "There were other files of course but not that one. Dr. Haston's was no longer there. I remember because I went looking for it when the R.C.M.P. officers showed up after the Dean took a leave-of-absence. It had disappeared!" The audience erupted at this disclosure. The intrigue was palpable.

Ms. Nelson returned to her seat while the audience digested this new disclosure. A bearded man made his way to a mic as the chatter died down. Blue jeans, leather sandals and a tweed sports coat gave away his status as a faculty member. "Hi. George Truscott from Philosophy. You mentioned that he was here for three years? Eventually became Chair? I notice your film was not critical of the people who let that happen. Don't you think some heads should have rolled on this?" There was more chatter. The moderator stood out from the wall where she had been leaning. She looked out nervously. Truscott's accusatory tone was alarming. Professor Wilson nodded affirmatively. He had an ally.

Daniel hesitated. He wasn't expecting to have to defend the University's decision to hire Haston nor was his intention of his film to critique it. He thought the fifty years that had elapsed would have smoothed the sharper edges from the scandal. He looked at the moderator for direction. He would have to respond. "Well. I mean...you raise a valid question. But, as the film pointed out he had done this type of thing at a hospital in Montreal as well, but under a different alias...and for five years!" He added a reasoned rebuttal to Truscott's charge. "He managed to fool a bunch of pretty smart people there too. He was good at what he did...but I suppose cleverness doesn't make him a good man. I hope the film wasn't insinuating that." The audience seemed mollified by this reminder.

The moderator received a signal that the next film was ready. Pleased for the diversion from the audience's hostile tone, she began her transition to the next film when a woman in the second row put up her hand. Before the moderator had a chance to intervene, the woman stood and began to speak. She was dressed neatly in a smart pant suit. Her hair was grey, elegantly styled, swept back fashionably making her appear her age but still clutching on to a youthful spirit. "You make him sound like he was trying to trick people! Dupe them!" There was a quake in her voice. "I was a student of his." She let that announcement dissipate. "I reject the insinuation I was fooled." The moderator looked around the room surveying the impact this change of course portended. "I learned more from him than anyone else I had at this place even if his credentials were phony." Conrad Wilson twisted in his seat to get a better look at her. He cast a stern glance and then signaled to his wife that they should go. A subtle shake of her head suggested an early exit would be imprudent and he sagged back in his seat. The woman continued to gush effusively. "In fact, I knew several students who thought the same thing!"

The old man who came late scratched the few errant hairs left on his grizzled chin, missed from his morning shave. He leaned forward and cocked his head to the side, straining to hear better.

More time had elapsed than was expected and the moderator, feeling she must move things along, began the introduction of the next film. Out of the corner of her eye she noticed Kelly pointing to the mic at other side of the room. There was another question.

"Well," with a forlorn sigh, "Okay. One last question."

"Sorry," the young man apologized. "I'm jus start'n...freshman." He adjusted his ball cap and donned a juvenile smile. "Haven't got a major yet," he joked. With a mischievous smile he added, "pisses my parents off." His attempt at humour trailed off into the void. He fumbled in his jeans pocket, pulling out a crumpled bit of paper. "Ah, ya...here it is. I wrote my question down." Smoothing the wrinkles he began to read, "If Haston were still alive...", he paused to look up at Daniel for confirmation, "...you said he'd be in his eighties right?" Daniel nodded. The young man continued, "If Haston were still alive, who'd he be now, I mean would he be like he was at first? Y'know...before he decided to become an imposter."

It could have been that the audience was saturated. It could also have been that they discounted the question given the juvenile nature of the questioner. Or, it could have been the concussive impact of the young man's seemingly innocuous question that gave rise to the crushing silence that ensued. It lingered longer than it should. Daniel was paralyzed to respond as he mulled the question over. *Had he missed the essential question* he thought. *What version of himself could Haston return to?*

Finally the moderator broke the silence. "Kelly, can you kill the lights please?" She looked at the young man benignly, "Sorry. We have to move on."

The old man who had come late gathered his cane and clumsily pushed his way out to the isle. He shuffled toward the door leaving behind the smudged brochure on his seat. Few noticed.

Liar, Liar, Pants on Fire

Just after the tracks Ted thought. He drove a bit more and then doubled back thinking he may have missed it. *That kid and his bull-shit stories* he mumbled while straining to find more clues. It was early in November and a cold east wind whipped newly spawned snowflakes into a dance of erratic swirls in front of Ted's windshield. Paulo had told him that the house was back a bit from the road and he warned that he might not be able to see it right off. His directions were vague and it was this inexactness that fueled Ted's suspicion. Coming up on his right was a small opening in the dogwood bushes. It looked like it might have been a driveway at one time. *Just wide enough for the Corolla* he thought. Nudging his way along he winced as the branches scraped the side of his nearly new car. Within a short distance from the road the greying features of what had once been a white house came into view. It was an awkward looking structure. The main part of the building appeared taller than it was wide. Tacked on to the back was an extra room that sagged to one side causing the eye some discomfort. Ribbons of black tar-paper fluttered from exposed spaces where siding once was. A rickety barn stood just beyond the house and the few faded red boards, still clinging to wind-battered beams, did little to hide its contents. The harsh barking from angry dogs announced his arrival. The details were beginning to line up. *Maybe there's some truth to this after all,* he thought.

He stopped just short of the house, unsure of where the driveway ended. A dirt path led up to a tired old door, cracked and blistered from years of neglect. A rusted screen attached loosely to the door frame—its mesh well-patched, quilt-like with several generations of screen threaded on. A considerable gap where the screen failed to connect to the frame made him wonder what purpose the screen door actually served. Ted could see recently made foot prints etched in the thin layer of snow that had now formed. They led from the house toward the barn where dogs were barking. A bike leaned against the jutting arm of a rusted farm implement anchored in the dirt. *It must be Paulo's* he thought.

There was menace in the dogs' tone so Ted felt it safer to check the house first before going to the barn. As he turned back toward the house the door began to open. It stuck part way, requiring an extra heave to get it to open all the way. A short-statured woman appeared in the opening staring out from behind the screen. As he got closer her features became clearer. She was older, maybe mid-seventies. A faded red ball cap hinted a youthful eagerness that competed with her age. The amber glow from her cigarette pulsed excitedly in the wind. She stared at him as he walked up.

"Hi." Ted waited for her to respond but none came. Not even a smile. "I may be in the wrong place...I'm looking for Paulo?" A pause lingered so he added, "Paulo Sanchez?"

She cocked her head to look around him toward the car and then back to him again. "Vhy?"

"Do you know him?" Ted inquired. She offered a subtle nod but said nothing. *She knows him!* he thought. He continued. "He mentioned that he worked with dogs ...and uh...he gave me directions to this place." He could detect no change in her affect. Ted continued cautiously. "I thought I'd stop by and see him."

Slowly, she pushed the screen door open and stepped out on to the threshold. She wore a frumpy sweatshirt with a prominent grease stain blotted in to the *Don's Autoparts* logo. A grimy blaze-orange scarf, the kind hunters wear, was wrapped loosely around her neck. Stiff brown pants rolled up at the cuff gave the appearance they were holding her thin frame upright rather than the other way around. Dirty tennis shoes worn through at the toes, one with binder twine for a shoe-lace, conveyed a practicalness bordering on eccentricity.

"See? Vhut you mean...see?" she demanded.

"Well uhm," Ted groped for some alternate phrasing. "See *HIM* I meant...he said he works with dogs...sled-dogs?" Ted expected this would end it. Her abrupt denial would give him what he came for, something he could confront Paulo with later. However, even after a long pause, there was no rebuff from her.

"Heeze nut here," was all she offered. A puff of wind tufted the hair around her wrinkled mouth as she spoke. Her cigarette pulsed brighter. She continued to stare at him.

Sensing his attempt at divining the truth from this old woman was faltering he added. "Oh. I see." He looked back at the barn and then at her. "Would you be Renate by any chance?"

"Who'vr you?"

"Oh...I'm a friend of Paulo's...Ted Watson...from Paulo's school."

"A friend?"

Regretting his choice of words, he corrected himself. "Well no...a counsellor actually."

"Yer not friend?"

Ted was feeling increasingly uncomfortable. He changed the conversation back to dogs. "Paulo told me that I could come and see him working with the dogs. He said you are helping him train them?" Ted waited for her to show signs of confusion. He thought the formality and discipline implied by the word 'train' would expose Paulo's conjure for what it was yet her face revealed no confirmation of his suspicion.

The wind picked up again, vibrating a loosened piece of siding. Her eyes blinked and the tightness drained from her face although her tone remained stern. "Eeze cold. Come. Inside." She moved the screen door a little wider, beckoning Ted to enter.

"No. It's all right. I don't want to bother you. I really just came to see how Paulo was doing." Renate stared at him but said nothing. He felt examined. A polite retreat was not an option. "Yeah. Sure...just for a minute." He didn't like the feeling. Control of the situation had shifted.

Renate led Ted through a hallway, narrowed by canyons of boxes and bundled newspapers. Dust and cobwebs were everywhere. He passed an opening to what must have been the living room. It was difficult to tell as all the furniture was occupied holding everything from coats to small appliances. A single shelf displayed a half-dozen pictures. Renate kept walking toward the back of the house and on into a kitchen area. A whiff of spoiled food and smoldering cigarettes greeted him as he emerged into the room. A cluttered table with a lonely turquoise chair, scarred and chipped, occupied most of the space in the tiny kitchen. A can of half-empty beans stood next to the stove, its jagged lid sticking up menacingly. Ted had difficulty imagining the tool used to open it. A blackened kettle sat askew, not quite centered on the burner. Stains around the sink and across the counter top formed a kind of mosaic record of past meals—*prepared in solitude most likely* Ted thought.

Renate moved a few things around as if she were searching for something. She picked up a cup and examined it. She removed her cigarette and placed it on the edge where the counter met the sink. Several brown burn marks already branded into the yellowed patina of the arborite surface suggested this was common practice. Blowing debris out of the bottom of the cup she asked, "Tea?"

"Ah...no thanks."

Renate looked at him plainly. Ted felt the need to justify his response. "I'm a coffee drinker," he lied.

"I make coffee fer you". It was not hospitality she conveyed.

"No. It's quite all right. I uh...I've had too much coffee today already." Her steady stare challenged the veracity of his claim.

Renate moved over to the stove and turned on a burner. She repositioned the kettle and then peeked to check its contents. "Paulo tell you bout Iditarod?"

Her question startled Ted. He nervously shifted his weight to the other leg. His plan to unveil Paulo's unfathomable story was unravelling at a faster pace than he could manage.

"Yeah...he kinda mentioned it."

"And you here to see if true." Her tone was resolute...not a question.

The abruptness of her assertion left him increasingly unsettled. Renate turned to face Ted. Her eyes, although deeply hooded with folds of sagging skin, still managed to pierce the thin veneer of his intent. He could not be evasive. She would know.

"Well, yes ...I guess," he responded. "He's been getting in trouble at school lately. You know...fighting...that kind of thing." He paused to take stock his assuaging was having. He continued cautiously. "This story he's telling about the Iditarod...I mean it seems ...well...far-fetched...you know...especially around here thousands of miles from Alaska?" There was no turning back. He anticipated her complicity in the lie would soon emerge. Renate remained quiet. Nudging further he added, "Kids'll make stuff up... you know...sometimes...who knows why...and other kids ...well...they can be mean." He waited for her to jump in. She didn't. Shame ping ponged back to him. He offered a final faltering defense. "I wanted to give Paulo a way out."

"Vhey out?" Her eyes bored into him.

Ted rephrased. "I mean ...a way out...you know...in case his story wasn't exactly true."

The heat from the burner caused the kettle to clink louder, interrupting the moment. Ted was thankful for the distraction. Renate switched her attention to the tea. She moved a few pots aside in the sink and pulled up a couple of sopping wet tea bags and plunked them into the kettle. Placing the lid on firmly and affixing the spout-whistle she turned abruptly to look at him and in doing so, inadvertently knocked a spoon to the floor. As she stooped to pick it up, her scarf drooped down revealing what it had meant to conceal. Ted's eyes grew with astonishment. The gap exposed a large growth protruding at an angle from her willowy neck. An angry scar ran the full length of the fleshy mound. It was not seeping but the bulge looked raw and chaffed, pushing out uncomfortably like a misplaced pregnancy. Ted pretended that he hadn't noticed.

"A dream come true. Heard of vhat Mr. Vhatson?"

Ted contemplated her question. "Sure? I guess?"

"I vunder bout the verd 'true' in them words…like 'true' and 'dream'…vhey don't belong together," she said as if trying to follow her own logic.

Ted's palms began to perspire. His bowels turned watery. "I …don't think I ever thought about it that way before." He glanced over his shoulder to the hallway that led to the front door. "I really should be heading …"

Renate wouldn't let him finish. "Vhen Mr. Vhatson? Vhen does duh dream become not a true thing…a lie?" Her question had an urgency to it. She wouldn't let him go without an answer.

"I'm uh…I'm not sure…I…I guess if the dream isn't…isn't realistic then it starts out as a kinda lie…maybe a lie to yourself? Is that what you are looking for?"

Renate's eyes danced with excitement at Ted's response. "Sit for minute Mr. Vhatson…vhanna show you someth'n." Renate pushed the chair toward him. The passion in her expression told him it would be imprudent to refuse. He nervously took the chair and sat down. Renate shuffled out of the room, her pants rubbing like pieces of sandpaper. She returned with a photograph that Ted guessed to be one of the ones he had spotted on the way in. She used the sleeve of her sweatshirt to clean it before placing it reverently on the table.

"This my Heinz."

Ted picked up the picture to get a closer look. It was taken on a sunny winter day. The terrain was flat and treeless, possibly on a frozen lake. There were a few mountains in the background. The scene was of a man with a thick beard and dark sunglasses. He was kneeling beside a large sled-dog with one arm holding the dog's neck in an affectionate embrace. Other dogs were in the picture as well. Leather traces led out of view toward what must have been a sled.

"Heinz?" he asked. Renate didn't say anything. She smiled and gave a noticeable exhale. A trail of tobacco-breath wafted between them. "Heinz is your...husband?"

Renate paused. An affectionate smile came across her face as she looked at the picture. "My boy...not husband...he's my boy."

Ted looked at the photo more intently. He tried to judge the age of it but it had faded and was quite wrinkled making it difficult to determine its provenance. *This could have been anybody* he thought. *Was she just imagining this?* This thinking roused some fear. *Was this some kind of psychosis?* "Oh. I see. He does sled-dog racing?" his voice trailing off.

"Use to," she replied. Renata kept staring at the picture. "He died." Her words were vacant, lacking any hint of emotion. "Picture vuz taken couple a'days b'for. Dogs ...everyth'n...all gone. I vuz vait'n for him to finish in Nome. Ten more hours...vhut is all. Vood have made it if ice didn't break through. He vuz in eight place."

Ted started to see where her discussion about dreams came from. "He was in the Iditarod?"

She looked up from the picture, offering a slight nod of affirmation. A shudder of apprehension gripped him as thoughts of Paulo's part in her story plunged through him like a rock through a window. *Where was this going* he thought. Just then the steam from the kettle began to whistle, demanding some attention. She put the picture down, went over to the stove and poured herself a cup of the boiling broth. Leaving it sit, she returned to her smoldering cigarette, its long ash falling to the floor as she placed it back in the corner of her mouth. "Yeah. Thirty five years. Few months it be thirty six. Vee use'duh train for it...very hard you know."

The smoke from her cigarette formed a mysterious shroud around her wrinkled face. The oddness of the image stopped Ted from probing for more information. Silence settled in the room like flakes of soft snow until a renewed round of barking broke the moment. Ted could hear faint shouting off in the distance. Renate looked up and then moved to the window. She wedged her fingers into the venetian blinds, dislodging a small puff of dust.

"He's back," she mumbled as if speaking to herself.

"Back?" Ted went to join her at the window. He was not prepared for what he saw. In the distance the steamy breath of several dogs frantically pulling a mud-spattered ATV came into view. Gravel and snow spit up from the dog's churning paws while hot lolling tongues lapped up the cool fall air. As the team got closer he could see Paulo clutching the steering wheel, his face locked in stolid concentration. Ted's eyes followed him as he adeptly brought the make-shift sled closer to the house. Shouts of "Easy! ...Gee! Gee!" and the breathy grunts of the dogs passing close by the window left Ted transfixed. He continued to track the team's progress as Paulo navigated the tight turn that led to the barn. The image of an ardent young handler in complete command of his exuberant charges clashed wildly with the Paulo he thought he knew. Ted glanced at Renate. Her face had a curious glow to it—*subdued pride perhaps...maybe more*...he couldn't be sure. He was about to say something but thought better of it.

The moment lingered until she retrieved her cup of tea from the counter and took the seat Ted had just vacated. She gave a long pull on her cigarette, coughed briefly and then took a sip. A noticeable tremor caused its contents to spill slightly, adding to the other stains on her sweatshirt. As she sat there in the plainness of her kitchen, her blank face prompted renewed contemplation. Ted wondered if she was despairing about what now seemed obvious to him. He looked at her scarf. A slight gape had opened enough for him to catch another glimpse of the tight bulge of skin extending from her throat. *The scarf, such an odd vanity* he thought. *From whom did it shield her fate* he wondered.

He turned back to Renate. "Does he know?"

Renate looked up. "Know vhut?"

"I mean ...does he know how ..." Holding his doubtfulness in check, Ted thought better of what he was going to say so he stopped.

"How realistic ...? Ain't that vhut you mean Mr. Vhatson?" Renate locked eyes with Ted's. She took another drag on her cigarette and then returned to the picture of her son. She held it affectionately, her thumb rubbing dust from his grizzled face, her lips trembling slightly and her eyes welling up. She raised her hand to the scarf and while giving it a few soothing strokes she answered his unfinished question with one of her own. "Who dizides Mr. Vhatson? Who?"

Her simple question sucked the oxygen out of the room. He had come to Renate's place to relieve a young boy from his own delusions and in doing so, claim victory over the truth. Instead he found the embryo of a truer tale, one more worthy of its telling, yet one hopelessly hobbled with unconquerable obstacles. Although he considered his motive noble enough at the time, now he felt like an intruder. Doubt had guided him to this place, like a bee to a false flower. There was no triumph to be had here. He had trespassed on these two people's lives and through the misguided force of his own compulsion he was leaving behind deep clodding footprints, having disturbed the soil of their shared hope.

"I better go." He waited a moment out of reverence but he did not expect her to respond. "I should say hello to Paulo before I head out." He went down the cluttered hallway to the door. It stuck as he tried to open it. An extra heave sprung it loose. He looked back one last time and then left. Renate did not look up.

The Empty Seat

The first thing you need to know'bout me is that a lot of shit goes on in my mind, stuff y'wouldn't get from the way I look and sound. I hear 'retard' a lot. But I'm not. I think I'm actually kinda smart but it's the kinda smart that isn't real obvious. You see I was born with CP so my speech is all breathy, spastic-sound'n—not even close to what I'm think'n, what I want others to understand. Face gets contorted as hell when I try to talk. Looks weird to most people I guess. Can't write worth a damn either...hands shake all over the place. So how am I write'n this stuff? That's what you're think'n isn't it? Well, I'm not. It's really Brinks and me talk'n. He listens to me think'n. He kinda takes it all in, even though he's not a real person ...feelings and shit. Complex stuff too. Sounds crazy I know.

Brinks has been a part of me for as long as I can remember but I never decided on his name till'bout a year ago. It was right in front of Doug's. Doug runs a barber shop across from the bank. I sell stuff from a cart next to his barber pole. When sales are slow, which they always are, I sit and watch for the Brinks truck. It usually comes'bout the same time every day. I love those trucks—always clean, sturdy look'n. They got strong stuff all around them like bars and shit. The windows are bullet-proof...tires look like they could run over a road full of jagged metal and still stay hard. Rugged. I like that. The way money goes in and out of them trucks is neat too—all secure with guards watch'n while a guy on the inside gives a guy on the outside bags of money. I think they have a special way of signal'n, a code or someth'n to let them know the coast is clear. I'm like the guy on the inside with all the valuable stuff and Brinks is like the guy on the outside. He takes the valuable stuff from me and delivers it. We have that special signal, not spoken words, just thoughts. That's why Brinks is a good name for him. He knows what I'm think'n without ever hav'n to say, 'pardon' or 'I didn't quite get that.' With Brinks I'm kinda like a whole person.

Doug's okay. I mean he helps me set up and stuff. 'Let's set you up over here,' he says. That's code for 'I don't want you too close to my customers'. I'm yoosta shit like that, doesn't bother me much. He's nice enough to let me be there I guess. I've been chased away a few times from different places. Tony Longo sells vegetables and fruit and stuff on the corner. He's got a cart too, only he doesn't have CP. He's a normal guy. 'Get da hell outta here…don't want you scaring my customers'. That's what Tony says if I set up too close to him. Brinks and I think he's an asshole but he's not phony'bout it. He tells you how he's feel'n, no code. Jus straight up truth. Don't get me wrong, Tony's mean but he tells a kinda truth—a mean truth—whereas Doug's kinda nice even though it's phony. It's funny that, the truth being mean and phony being nice. I guess phony's better than the truth sometimes. It's weird shit like that that messes me up. My problem is I can't be mean or nice. I have to be neutral all the time cuz if I get too worked up'bout stuff all hell breaks loose and no one knows what I'm feel'n or try'n to say…c'ept my brother. He always knew.

I got a cool cart to sell my stuff. My brother made it for me for my 21st birthday. 'This'll keep you out of the bars' he joked. It's a box with wheels. It has a handle with a spring-loaded lever so when I push on it, the brake releases and it rolls. If I don't push it, the brake stays on. It's good for guy like me cuz my hands can't squeeze leavers like on normal bike brakes. The box has a flip top that becomes a shelf when it's open. The side has a bench that folds down for me to sit. The cart has a plastic pipe. I stick an umbrella in it that I found in a garbage can. It's more for the sun than the rain cuz no one buys stuff in the rain. Like I say, it's pretty cool. Makes me feel independent.

I'm a business man…sort of. I sell leather stuff with colored vinyl thread looped though pre-drilled holes…pencil cases and wallets and shit like that. My brother made a deal with CDC. It's a sheltered workshop that makes simple stuff, y'know made by retarded folks. 'Did you make this yourself?' customers ask. I don't exactly lie, just push out a grunt and a droopy smile. They think it's a 'yes'. If they thought I said 'no' they probably wouldn't buy it so I don't try to correct them. They wouldn't understand me anyways. It's a bit phony I guess but like I say, things seem to work better with phony than they do with the truth. I wonder why they buy my stuff sometimes. I mean there is classier stuff in the stores...and cheaper too. I guess it makes them feel good buying from a cripple and all. 'Oh this? Yeah. It's my new wallet...bought it from the crippled guy down the street.' It's nice that they buy from me and all but like I say, I seen better stuff at Walmart.

I'm wait'n for Trevor. He's gonna wheel me into the Coliseum tonight. The Bulldogs are play'n. My brother got some tickets a while ago and t'night's the night. Trevor's a guy who swims with me at the Y once a week. I don't really swim...just float around with some water wings on...y'know, the kind the kids wear. I kinda like it even though it's fake. It makes me feel like I'm swim'n. I like bee'n in the water. Ever notice how a body looks weird when half of it is under water? Refraction I think they call it. The neat thing is my body doesn't look that weird when I'm in the water cuz my body looks like everyone else's. Funny that, the swim'n pool make'n everyone look like me. I tried tell'n that to Trevor once but he didn't get it.

Trevor gets me into my suit and stuff at the pool. I could do it myself but I'd have to be on the floor and it's all wet from people showering and stuff. It's kinda embarrass'n have'n someone pull down your pants so they can put a bath'n suit on you...you know, two grown men in a public place...probably doesn't seem right to a lot of people. That's a feel'n I'm used to too...have'n to do stuff that doesn't seem right to some folks. Trevor ain't comfortable though. I can tell. He keeps his arms soldier-straight when he's do'nit—doesn't want to give the wrong impression I guess.

Trevor and I talk sports after swim'n...well, he talks and I listen cuz I don't talk so good. I guess he thinks it's better than silence, but I'm okay with silence...hav'n a conversation is exhausting for me. Get'n the words out is hard enough but when you gotta repeat a few times...well that's a whole other level of frustration. Lucky for me I have Brinks to talk to.

First time I met Trevor was in the restroom at the Y. I fell in one of the cubicles while I was try'n to pull up my pants. Trevor heard me thrash'n around, maneuvr'n to get under the stall door. There I was roll'n on the floor, pants down to my ankles. Hell'uv'a way to meet a guy right? Anyways after that Trevor worked someth'n out with Louise and now we swim every Tuesday night. I remember him say'n, 'I'll do my lengths while you float around' when we set th'rangement up. I guess he was try'n to make me feel like it wasn't charity, y'know, like it's not an inconvenience for him cuz he was goin to do it anyways but I was pretty bummed when he said it. I was kind'a hope'n he'd swim with me...y'know, normal friend stuff. He's nice enough for doin it I guess but still...

I know Trevor doesn't want to take me to the game ta'night. He was kinda phony'bout it when I phoned. 'It's Ron...the guy I swim with,' I could hear him say'n to his wife. 'I think he wants me to take him to the hockey game...something about his brother?' 'Brother? You never mentioned he had a brother,' I could hear her say'n. He didn't even try to muffle the receiver, sort of a whisper-talk. A lot of people think if you can't speak good then you can't understand good either. 'Gee I don't know Ron...as much as I'd like to see the game...getting away for the whole afternoon and evening would be hard for me.' That's code for 'I don't really want to go. He probably didn't believe I could pull it off. I mean this is complicated stuff arrang'n for a wheelchair van and all that shit. How could a guy like me make this happen, right? I betch'a he was surprised as hell when he phoned Louise... y'know, expect'n her to tell him I was make'n it all up or sumth'n.

Trevor's like that sometimes, kinda doubtful'bout shit. He embarrassed me one time at the Y. I brought some of my stuff to sell after swim'n and I was show'n it to him. 'Wow! You made this stuff yourself.' He wasn't ask'n it like it was a question, if y'know what I mean, not like he wanted an answer. Suspicious I guess. I could'a tried splain'n it all to him but he wouldn't understand me even if I did. 'It's just that ugh...getting that vinyl into those holes...well that must be hard...you can do that with your hands?'. I can still see him shaking his head. 'You'll have to show me sometime.' Firstly, I never said I made them myself. Secondly, even if I did say I made them myself, why should I have to prove it to him? There's a word for that shit...I think it's *demeaning* or something like that...makes you feel crappy, second-class or someth'n. Most friends would pick up on that shit...y'know, hurt feelings and stuff, but I don't show embarrassment that good...my face, it doesn't work like normal people's so I guess it's hard for others to figure out what I'm feel'n. You'd have to know me I guess to know I was upset. My brother could always see it in my eyes...wouldn't have to cry or noth'n. He just knew.

Anyways Trevor agreed to be my escort for ta'night. *Escort*. I hate that word...feels like I'm goin to a church dance or someth'n. But it's what the agency calls it. I need a wheelchair for the game. I usually do okay with crutches but with it being winter and the Coliseum being crowded and stuff it's better if I'm in a chair. Besides, when I walk with crutches my face gets all twisted and contorted from the effort. I guess it kinda freaks people out. Legs flail all over the place too. 'Praying mantis legs', my brother used to tease.

Jamie got me ready 'bout forty minutes ago so I'm kinda hot sit'n in the apartment all bundled up. She did me first, then she started work'n on Mike. He's my roommate. Mikes 'bout ten years older than me. He and I have a bit of a crush on Jamie. She's got nice boobs and she's kinda all over us when she's get'n us dressed and stuff. Smells nice too...her hair and stuff. Sometimes her cheek touches mine when she is lean'n over...smell tobacco on her breath. It's almost like we are kiss'n. She's got a boyfriend so I don't make a move on her. But I feel like it.

There's a knock at the door. "That must be your escort...what's his name...Tom?"

"Uhhhmf TwwwVRR."

"Oh ya. Trevor." Jamie takes a few steps toward the door.

"Hi. Have I the right apart..."

"Trevor?"

"That's right. Is this Ron's place?"

"Yep. Right place. I'm Jamie, Ron's CLA. I was just getting him and Mike ready."

"CLA?"

"Sorry. Community Liaison Assistant." Jamie rolls her eyes while she says it. "They're in here."

Trevor comes in all smile'n. "Hey buddy. Ready for the big game?" Ya'd think he was look'n forward to it.

"TTTTTkkkkSS ehhnn POWWTs."

Trevor looks at Jamie and shrugs.

"He's telling you he has the tickets in his pouch. I think there's six, right Ron?" Jamie checks the list.

"Six! I thought it was just Ron and I?"

"Nope. The van's almost full...pretty much the whole floor is going."

"Floor?"

"Oh. I assumed you knew this. This whole floor is an IL." Trevor squints a bit. Jamie clarifies, "... *Independent Living*, you know, adults with disabilities? I think Sean is the only one not going. Is that right Ron?"

"Hhhumph."

Trevor's stand'n in front of our full-length closet-mirror. I could see the whole scene with him look'n on at Mike and me lined up ready to go, the two of us all bundled up with my toque look'n like a sock on a watermelon—hate it when Jamie leaves it like that but I can't pull it on myself—and then Mike, slouch'n in his chair, head roll'n around like a rusty can propped up on a stick. What a sight he must think! Trevor looks like he just got punched in the gut.

"I ugh...I didn't know...ugh, the lady...on the phone?"

"Louise? She's the Case Manager."

"Right. Louise. I thought it would be just he and I." Trevor's eyes are all pinched in, intense like. "I guess I should've checked...didn't know there'd be more...six you said?"

Jamie nods.

"Just me?"

"No. Well ... sort of. Mike's escort was supposed to come but cancelled at the last minute. There's Yaz the van driver, and Isaac, Barry's buddy. He can help out."

"Yes. But you said six and that's only three adults?"

"*Escorts*, you mean *escorts*, every one is an adult on the IL." Jamie corrected. Jamie's cheeriness was disappear'n quickly. "The others are ambulatory...except Al. He's got a power chair."

"But you said disabled?"

"Well, they have other needs...other than physical I mean. But they aren't children." Jamie sounds a bit harsh like she was scold'n him. "Anyway, we're a bit late. Yaz will be angry with us. You push Ron and I'll bring Mike up the rear."

———

Trevor has just wheeled me into the lobby. Jamie's follow'n behind with Mike. Everyone is here 'cept Al. I hate that guy. What a dick-head. If it wasn't for my brother, Al wouldn't be cum'n with us. 'Here,' I remember him say'n. 'They're for everyone on the floor,' he said when he handed me the tickets. 'Yes, even Al!' He could read my mind.

A few minutes go by while we wait for Al. Trevor is shift'n his weight from one foot to the other kinda nervous like. Jason is talk'n to Bernice, jabber'n away like he usually does, silly stuff. Jason looks okay from behind but once he turns around you get quite a shock.

"Hi. Jason's the name, hav'n fun's the game." He holds out his hand for Trevor to shake it. Trevor flinches. Jason's hand is hang'n in mid air, wait'n for Trevor to oblige.

"Hi ugh...Trevor. I'm ugh...with Ron...you going to the game I guess?" His eyes are dart'n from side to side like a pinball but keep snap'n back to Jason's face. Jason had a gearshift go right through his cranium when he was seven years old...had to rebuild the left side of his face. The scars tell a horrible story. He's got a fake eye that doesn't move when his other one does. Looks weird as hell when you're not used to it. Face is a bit caved in too...sort'a like a horror movie guy. Jason's nice though. I actually like him. He's not phony. But, he's kinda stuck at seven years old...does stupid things like kids do even though he's in his thirties. Once Jamie's kid asked him to take out his fake eye...and he did! Grossed the poor little kid out...screamed like hell. Jamie gave him royal shit. He said he was sorry and stuff but guess what? When the kid asked him to do it again minutes later he took the gawddam thing out again! It's obvious that sumthinz wrong with his head...doesn't seem to get embarrassed or feel shamed'bout stuff he does. Jamie says Jason can't feel emotions the same way normal people do. That part of his brain is gone, the emotional part. I'm kinda envious'bout that. He grosses people out, not on purpose of course, but it doesn't bother him. I hate when people look at me the same way they look at Jason. Not all people. Just some. I wish it didn't bother me but it does. My brother and I yoosta talk'bout this a lot. He knew it bugged me. He yoosta point people out. 'See that guy over there...the guy with the red hair. How about the lady who served us coffee...notice the Aussie accent? Think they're embarrassed about being different? Hell no. Being different is cool to them. It's who they are man! You're different just like them. Different is cool. Celebrate it!', he'd say. I guess he was kinda right but still, it's hard.

The elevator door jus opened. Al comes roaring out with his gawdamn power chair. He's all decked out with leather pants and a leather jacket. He always wears that shit. If he wasn't such a dickhead I'd feel sorry for him. From the neck down nuth'n works. Says he used to be in a motorcycle gang...I mean even if it's true, act'n all tough and shit like that is a bit much. I sometimes wonder what he was like before the accident. He's got'a cool chair though...uses a sip-and-puff control to move it. It's the only way he can drive it cuz his arms and hands don't work. He's always run'n into people. Personally I think he does it on purpose cuz I never seen him run'n into chairs and stuff. He just seems to like ram'n people like he's mad or sumth'n. It's kinda funny cuz it pisses people off but they don't get mad at him? I mean the guy's got nuth'n from the neck down! People just say 'sorry' when they probably feel like saying 'watch it asshole'. I guess people are phony that way. I try to keep my distance from him but somedays he rams me, crutches and all. 'Outta the way gimp!' he mumbles. I tell him to fuck off when he does it but it doesn't come out right. Words get all garbled when I get worked up...my face gets red and the eyes bulge out but noth'n but a slobbery groan comes out'a my mouth. I must sound like a wounded cow. Al just laughs. I'd like to plow him but he can't really defend himself...wouldn't be a fair fight.

Yaz has started load'n up the van. Yaz's one of the Tender Care drivers. *Tender Care*! That's what they call it. Can you believe it? Sounds like a gawdamn diaper service! Yaz's been drive'n us around for years. 'Ah right...who first?' he says. Al goes first. He always goes first—drives right on to the lift even before Yaz gives the OK. "Easy Al. I shut yo shen off...only rum fer wen driver on dis tren," Yaz jokes while he locks Al's chair in place. Yaz's a pretty decent guy...not phony. He kids around with us all the time...kinda like friends do. Now it's Mike's turn. Jamie wheels him on to the lift.

"Okay Yaz. He's all yours." Jamie turns to Trevor. "This is Trevor by the way, Ron's escort. He's going to be Mike's escort as well tonight."

"Well...not...not exact..."

"Ah...I see." Yaz smiles, "Dew fer price a wen," he winks. "Betcha wesh Jamie tag'n long dun'ya Ron," Yaz whispers as he buckles me my chair. He gives me a wink. He winks a lot.

Mike's like me with CP but he's in a chair permanently...no crutches. He speaks better than I do though. We talk a bit. He kinda knows what I'm try'n to say...sorta fills in the gaps. It's like a CP thing. He has had more speech therapy than I have. I guess that's why he's better at it. That stuff never worked for me. I'm not sure why. My brother told me that they kinda gave up on it after mom died. 'Didn't stop you from swearing though,' my brother yoosta joke. Mike's chair has just been locked in and Trevor gets the OK to wheel me in beside him. I can smell the booze on Mike already. I don't say nuth'n cuz I think he might be a bit depressed.

Barry's next. He's got no legs or arms...bin like that since birth. Isaac is always with him. I yoosta think he was Barry's CLA but they're actually good friends! Can ya believe that? I mean Isaac's a normal guy. He's aboriginal...Ojibwa or someth'n. He's got long black hair that's braided at the back...wears a beaded necklace. They're artists. Isaac does photography and Barry's a mouth painter. He's pretty damn good at it too. He sells his stuff and not because he's crippled. Not like me. I think people would buy Barry's stuff even if they didn't know a crippled guy painted it. He's got stuff at a local art gallery. It's pretty shit-hot even for a regular painter...nature stuff. That one over there hanging in the lobby, the goldfinch, it's his...looks like a gawdamn photograph!

Anyway, they're both chain smokers. They always share a cigarette. Isaac holds it in Barry's mouth for a puff and then he takes a turn. I think that's neat...kinda like a total bond, not worried bout germs and shit. Trust. I mean it's a simple thing but it seems like true friendship to me. I envy them. I'll tell you a joke I been think'n bout. I feel like tell'n Barry that he should quit smok'n cuz it'll stunt his growth. Brinks and I laugh at this, cuz even if Barry had legs he still wouldn't be very tall. He'd be like a midget. It's a joke I wish I could tell him...you know, other than Brinks. Barry might even be the kinda guy who would laugh at it. He's solid enough to know I'd be kidding around with him. I don't like to chance it though in case it comes out wrong. I wouldn't mean any harm. I think Barry would know that but I can't be sure. I'd like to kid around with people if I could. I see people joke'n with each other...teas'n each other bout their faults. I'd like to be able to do that or let them do that to me, you know, in a good natured way. My brother and I used to kid all the time...not hurtful stuff...jus teas'n.

Bernice hesitates and then jumps in, whoop'n and cluck'n with her teeth like she always does. She's plunked herself down behind the driver's seat. "Any sirens Yaz...don't like sirens...no sirens okay Yaz." Bernice's okay but weird sometimes especially when there's loud noises. Yaz's good with her. "No. No t'nite Neecy. I tink you seff. I luk afer you if hare dum." Bernice sniffs the seatbelt before buckl'n herself in. Her eyes blink all the time, like one of them caution signs. Jamie says she's autistic whatever that is.

Yaz motions Trevor to sit beside Bernice. "Oh? I thought I might..." pointing to the passenger seat.

"No. Isaac sit dare. You here."

Trevor nods obediently and shifts in beside Bernice. He leaves a space between them.

"Shove over man," Jason blurts. Trevor looks at Yaz. Yaz nods. Jason doesn't wait, jus pushes himself into the seat next to Trevor, a big goofy grin on his face. Trevor glances nervously to the right. He's real close to the caved-in side of Jason's face. I could see him try'n not to stare...he looks like a trapped animal.

So there you have it. We are all in and head'n to the Coliseum. Ordinarily I'd be look'n forward to a night like ta'night. I'd been before...with my brother. It's kinda a fun night out for a guy like me even though I'm not much of a sports guy. Ya'know, the noise and the excitement and all but ta'night, I wasn't sure. I wasn't sure how I'd be.

———-

We're back. It's a little after midnight. Yaz just got Mike's chair off and he's taken him up the elevator with Al. Trevor and I are wait'n.

My emotions are still pretty raw cuz'a what happened. I mean there was the typical shit you'd expect with the gang I hang out with. Al barged right through security with his gawdamn chair. Yaz...I mean that guy's a saint...had to smooth things over with the cops so Al could get in. I was kinda hope'n they'd arrest him or kick'm out or sumth'n. What an asshole! Then there was Bernice. The Bulldogs won 8 to 6 which meant the horn blew eight frigg'n times sending her run'n out into the lobby hold'n her ears, scream'n like a banshee. Yaz had to get her out from behind one of the concessions at one point. Jason got in shit too. He asked the couple in front of him if he could have a handful of their popcorn. He must'a scared the shit out'a them cuz the guy and his girlfriend got up and left after they looked at him. Then there was Mike. He got a little tippsy which freaked Trevor out. I don't know why. I mean drunk CP isn't much different than regular drunks far as I can figure.

Like I say, things were okay...till that shit-head sat in my brother's seat. The way it works at the Coliseum is the wheelchair platform is nestled in with the real good seats. My brother's seat...he has a season's ticket...is right next to the space for wheelchairs. He bought that particular one so I could go with him to the game once in awhile...ya'know, sit side-by-side like normal people. Anyways, the ushers know where season's ticket holders sit cuz they see them all the time and if they notice an unfilled seat after the game starts, they assume the season's ticket holder isn't goin to show. So if a guy slips them a few bucks, they let a cheap-seat guy move up to a better one. Y'know, gives them a bit of extra cash. No big deal. Well ta'night that's what happened. Only it was a big deal. Someone plunked himself down in my brother's seat. That's when everything went south. First I tried to get him to move but it didn't go so well. I can still hear that shit head, 'What's your problem buddy! You're spill'n my GODDAMN beer for fuck sakes!' The angrier I got the less I could say stuff that made sense. As I said, this happens when I get worked up...and I got real worked up. Tried hit'n the guy. 'Jesus Christ! Can y'believe this fuck'n retard!' Beer spilled over the lady in front of him. Trevor must'a thought I was hav'n a fit or sumth'n...dragged my chair back to the lobby which pissed me off even more. The more he tried to calm me down, the more pissed I got. It wasn't pretty. I jus couldn't stand that guy sit'n in my brother's seat. I couldn't go back in...feel'n stayed with me the rest of the night.

So that's what happened. Now the night is over and we're here in the lobby of my apartment wait'n for the elevator. Trevor still hasn't said much about the incident.

"Look Ron...I'm sorry for ugh...for taking you away from the game. I didn't know what was happening." I jus look at him from the corner of my eye. I got a lot of trouble with eye-contact cuz my head doesn't always do what it's post'a. "Isaac, told me about the seat. I didn't know it was your brother's. I would've...I might'a been able to get the usher..." Trevor looks up at the floor indicator. The elevator seems stuck on the 5th floor. "I ugh, I didn't know...didn't know he died." He kept stare'n up at the number 5. "I wish..." He's try'n to say sumth'n but it doesn't come out.

The moment hangs in the air. He's still stare'n up at the floor indicator. Finally the 5 changes to a 4 and then to a 3. A moment later a ding alerts us that the door would be open'n. Yaz steps out. A whiff of vomit follows him.

"Mike he sick," Yaz pats his stomach, wince'n as he says it. "I cleanz hem up. Too much drink I tink." He winks at Trevor. Before he heads out the door, he stops and touches my arm. "Y'no worry Ron. Y'brutter knows you dare. He happy you saw game wit'm." Yaz points up to the sky as he says it. "Sides...Bulldogs won!", he winks again. Trevor doesn't say noth'n. He pushes me in the elevator and we head up to my apartment. He looks pretty beat up over the whole thing. Rosa, the night duty lady, is in Mike's bedroom wrestling with his soiled clothes. "Ah Mike! Why you do dis?", I could hear her scold'n. Trevor wheels me into the liv'n room, hands me my crutches. "Here", he says. He's kinda solemn like he's at a funeral or sumth'n. "See you Tuesday." He leaves clos'n the door behind him. I don't cry...but I feel like it.

About the Author

Joseph (Joe) Morin is a retired educator. Upon receiving his initial certification from Toronto Teacher's College (1970) he spent almost three full decades teaching K-12 in Ontario, mostly in the field of Special Education. He attended York University in Toronto as an undergraduate (B.A. Sociology, 1974), University of Toronto for his graduate degrees (M. Ed., 1976 and Ed.D., 1998). Upon retiring from K-12 in 1999, he taught at the University of Wisconsin – Eau Claire until 2014.

He currently resides in Calgary Alberta Canada with his wife of 54 years. He has one daughter, and two grandchildren.

He has had a long-standing interest in the writing process having published technical works in both professional journals and in a collection of curricular guides. Some of this discipline has been applied to his works of fiction but certainly not all. Fiction he finds, is a different animal and the feeling of still being a 'novice' writer in the midst of all his experience has been hard to shake. That being said, he enjoys the freedom fiction provides, freedom to explore different forms of expression while relieved from the shackles of technical writing.

He can be reached for comment at morinje@icloud.com.